CERNON

The Genesis of Paradigm Lost

R. Roderick Rowe

RWCollins Publishing

RWCollins Publishing
randyc@rwcollinspublishing.com

The characters and events in this book are fictitious. Any similarity to real persons, living or dead, is coincidental and not intended by the author.

This book contains mention of sexual situations and may not be appropriate for some audiences.

Printed in the United States of America

About the cover. The background image is presented as a public domain image as it is found on many public sites. It is a photo from France and the France Museum of History. The character used as Cernon is purchased with thanks from Deposit Photos as are the antlers.

From the Author

In this novella, you will find referrals to other tales and histories in the world of Paradigm Lost. Many of these other stories are already written and published. I'll give some more detail at the end of this work, so, for now, here is a simple list of other titles to look for in the world of Paradigm Lost.

Heretic, First stand-alone book of the Lost in Legend Series (July 2023)
The Sophia Shaman, Second stand-alone book of the Lost in Legend Series (Dec 2023)
The Sundering, Battle of the Founder's Grove, Third stand-alone book of the Lost in Legend Series (Sometime in the next year)

Jamari and the Manhood Rites, Book One of the Jamari and the Manhood Rites Trilogy
Jamari Shaman, Book Two of the Jamari and the Manhood Rites Trilogy
The Founder's Sons, Book Three of the Jamari and the Manhood Rites Trilogy

Eros Times, Book One of the Eros Times series
Night Studies, Book Two of the Eros Times series

Paradigm Lost is a world-story spanning tens of thousands of years including the formation of human history, pantheons of greater spirits, religions, and churches along with human love and hate. As a result, it will continue to grow with new titles as the author fills in further tales of how mankind came to share our planet with the Tuatha Dé Cernon.

Ancient Spirit

Founder: If the winds are buffeting Eagle away from His perch, Eagle finds a new perch to nest on.

Reader: You should write that down.

Founder: It is already written but no one has read it because it pushes them away from their perch.

Justin Earl Knight, *Founder of the Elk Creek Tribe*
***

Chapter One

The Sophia Shaman

Milltown Hill, near Yoncalla, state of Lincoln, USA 2163 CE

I offer this tale, hoping humankind can one day learn to live with the Founder's Paradox. Step away from comfort and embrace the paradox. Because it pushes you away from whatever place of comfort you've found for your spirit to cease its questing for answers.

The human spirit should never stop questing!
***

This tale should be closely kept and guarded. As it probably should be for all time. But there needs to be a version somewhere. Perhaps intended only for the Knight Shamans and the Sophia Shamans, as those positions advance from one individual to another. Even that limit, though, is almost frightening to comprehend should this tale reach the wrong ears! The revelations here are far beyond what mere mortals can comprehend, and even I, who lived through them, can't fathom what they mean to mankind and our future.

I leave in Cernon's hands the decision of who sees the tale.

Now is the time to tell of Cernon.

This tale goes so far in the distant past that there is no writing to be found, only faint scratching and etchings on cave walls. The Antlered Man first appeared somewhere between twenty and forty thousand years ago, depending on what source you believe. "These painters were storytellers with imaginations," is what we were told. Mankind could not know what it truly meant when we first stumbled across those depictions in the many cave systems in France, Spain, Belgium and so many other ancient lands.

The naysayers stipulated that these intricate paintings and bas-relief carvings represented horned beasts. As the food source of those ancient ancestors, that was the depictions' only meaning. The stag's head on a man's body only represents the importance of the deer to our ancestors, they said. Any who questioned just why ancient man would go to so much trouble to scribe such images into the rock itself were quickly silenced.

Yet we could trace the progression of the stag-man across the continents and eons.

A Shared Spirit Journey

There was an earlier journey with Cernon before the one I'll tell of here. One I had thought of as the most significant experience I would ever experience as a shaman. It was the first time he guided me into the past.

I joined in meditation with him from a quiet spot above the Founder's Glade. I let him lead as if he were a simple spirit guide who I had found in the Middle World instead of the greater spirit I knew him to be. During that first shared journey, he led me to a former tribe of people who herded elk in the American west. We went so far back that humans hadn't invented time yet. There was only "now" along with some remembrance of what had gone before. Very little thought to the dreams of any future outside of gathering and preserving foods for the next season.

He and I travelled with that far-past tribe for a full season, then Cernon led me home.

When I returned from that journey, I found that only an hour had passed. A half year of experience and travel for me, only a short span during my time.

"You keep expecting time to be the same in your Dream World as it is in the Other Worlds," Cernon admonished me. "Let me guide you to an even earlier epoch, so you can see what I mean."

Then He led me to His beginning. And, yes, I'm suddenly capitalizing when referring to Him. He may not be a Greater God, as the Creator God in Heaven or the Great Spirit, but after that journey, I recognize He is much more than I had ever known before!

During the Founder Knight's travel with the gods, Cernon had been his constant companion and guide. When the spirit of Founder Knight came to live within the tree he had designated for just that purpose, Cernon came home with him. When Cernon trod the paths of the Founder's Glade, he wore the aspect of an ancient stagman. He had huge antlers adorning his human head; a scraggly red-brown beard that seemed more like that of an adult bull elk than anything normally growing from human cheeks; and well over eight feet from cloven hoof to russet-maned crown, not counting those massive antlers.

I know I could not have done that journey absent His guidance, and I know I would never want to make it on my own for fear of not finding my way back. Or, as I think back on it, I may never want to make that journey again. Even with Cernon's help.

Chapter Two

Journey Through Time

"I would share with you my beginning time," Cernon said to me on another morning in the wood above Milltown Village. He, in his physical form, had only recently ventured away from the center of the Founder's Glade. He had become fond of visiting the Ancestor's Grove near our stronghold.

Even as I used the mycelium networks with Jamari in our earliest days, I still didn't understand their importance to Cernon's physical form in our world. We, as a tribe, had not intended to establish the mycelial network as a part of re-forming the temperate rain forest we built. The vast growth of mushrooms and their supporting mycelia were part and parcel of the growing forest, though.

"I would enjoy learning of your beginning," I answered Cernon, little aware that I would have a much closer introduction than I could have dreamed of. No human could have imagined that beginning!

"Take my hand, and don't let go, no matter what you see, feel, hear or sense," Cernon said as he reached down to me.

When I clasped that giant hand, it was like a small girl holding onto her father when crossing a busy street. Mind you, I was a full adult at 5' 6" but the height of our new benefactor dwarfed me.

I felt his grip tighten on my hand. Then the world swirled away.

This was no gentle slide down a sweeping tunnel as a journey to the Lower World. Instead, it was the sundering of my mind and body into a kaleidoscope of shattered prisms. Bright colors drowned out all other senses as they led in a roaring flight away from my essence and into some other reality. I instinctively tightened my already firm grip on Cernon. It was no longer to his calloused hand, though. Instead, I focused on holding onto our bond as the universe shredded around me. I deeply feared the eventual shredding of my self as every other thing tore apart around me. If I had possessed a heart in this quasi-existence, I'm sure it would have pounded itself into failure from sheer fright.

The time in that partial existence could have been an instant or an eternity, I could never recall which. I remember my relief when I emerged from chaos into a real world.

Mountains surrounded us. Each crowned in a snowy cap with icy capes trailing down their sides. I realized in that moment what glaciers were. The pristine pictures of ice floes from my studies earlier in life had misled me. These were elemental powers, large, blinding, and all-encompassing. There was no way out of this valley without scaling a wall of ice, it seemed.

I shivered in reflex before realizing that the magic in the portal had somehow clothed me in softened furs. These were wooly pelts fashioned into parka and trous, and thick boots strapped onto a set of snowshoes. We hadn't simply traveled from my home to this ethereal place, but had somehow become a part of it as well. Beside me Cernon, who steadfastly remained unclothed in our world and time, contemptuous of the prissy disdain of nudity left over from the before-the-fall days, was clad in thick layers of furs. I couldn't even imagine the animal big enough and wooly enough to provide that parka. I looked up and into his eyes.

"Gulp," I blurted out in a failed attempt to talk. My shock overcame me and I collapsed to the ground.

"It was a very arduous journey," he reassured me as he sat down and cradled my head in his lap. "You'll be yourself shortly. Just relax and look around at the world as it was in my beginning."

I looked as directed. Once I got past the stunning scale of the surrounding mountains, I saw we were just above a small stream which meandered its way through a twisting draw of trees. To me, it felt like the severest of mid-winter, yet I could see leafy buds emerging from the trees and shrubs. There was a hum of insects in the air and somehow a liveliness I would never have expected in the gentle hills of the state of Lincoln. Even considering further north where Oregon was, with snow-capped Mount Hood, there was nothing like this. If I were to have drawn an Alpine Mountain scene, this would have been it.

I heard a hubbub of voices from around a bend in the stream and turned to watch as a small gathering of men foraged their way up the streamside. They were gathering small tubers from the grassy areas. These men wore furs, though not furs as I had seen. Instead of cured, it seemed this tribe had beaten the skins into softness as they hung in the air, then draped them about their bodies. The hair of these nomads was black as coal and tangled. The whorls held bracken and leaf as if they had woven them into decorative patterns. One or two had sea shells pierced and strung into their locks as well. Each of them sported a scraggly beard on somewhat lesser chins.

I struggled to my feet, still shaky from the shock of the journey, then looked at Cernon to see if we should greet them. He motioned me to silence, then pointed as if to say "watch." As they approached, I became concerned that they would walk right over us, then I realized they didn't see us at all. When one passed right through Cernon, I found we were less than a spectral presence to them.

When they passed up the valley, Cernon and I turned to follow.

"Where are we?" I asked quietly.

"A better question could be 'when' are we?" was Cernon's cryptic answer.

I looked up into his eyes to gauge whether he was jesting with me. He looked serious, though.

"We have passed back to a time before humans bound themselves into the very construct of 'time'. Before they first envisioned a 'tomorrow'," he said. "For these people, they can visit their past in memory at will. But 'tomorrow' is only a faint possibility and 'day-after-tomorrow' is almost as imaginary as 'next week'."

I considered this quandary as we continued to follow the troop of gatherers. When the grassy areas transitioned into a rocky bank, they stepped right into the stream and began turning over rocks. The gatherers swooped up several walking-twig insects to put in their leather bags. Then there was a celebration as they pulled a couple of crayfish from the depths. Apparently, they would eat better with this fare than on other nights. They discovered more crayfish as they turned their full attention to this new find.

Further up the draw, they turned away from the stream and climbed a cliff face. The group disappeared behind a small copse of evergreens. Cernon and I followed along. We found a small opening in the cliff. Cernon crawled in on hands and knees, holding his antlered head so his tines lay along his spine. I could travel fully upright, though taller than the tallest of the gatherers.

When the space opened enough to stand, we watched the last of the gatherers file into an opening further inside the maw of the entry. Flickering firelight danced along the darkened rocks. Cernon stood as he entered the larger area. We watched the travelers greeted by women and children in the light of several hearth fires placed around the perimeter of a cave dwelling.

One woman stepped forward from the shadows, raising her hands for attention. "Welcome home," she said in a language I understood in my mind but which was garbled in my ear. The speaker was ageless, somehow both young and old at the same moment. Her hair was long and scraggly like the rest, with not a touch of grey. Her recessed chin sported a sparse outburst of fine hairs which highlighted her expressive lips. She waved her hands in emphasis as she spoke, and I realized that the hand placements and movements were an integral part of the language. "I have seen that you carry enough food for us all, and I have seen that the deer are coming soon. Let us feast tonight, for tomorrow we prepare for the hunt."

Chapter Three
Meeting the Tribe

I watched as other women set flagon-bags of water to hang from tri-pods of sticks. They then placed heated rocks from the fires into these bags, producing steaming, hissing spouts. When the rocks had given up their heat, spoon-like sticks were used to fish them out, then they dropped others in. Once the water maintained a strong wafting of steam, they dropped the tubers and grubs in for cooking. The few crayfish had their own pot, into which the cooks dropped them with some sense of relish and celebration.

The youngsters, none younger than six or seven, sat in rings around the various hearth-fires, staring at the pots in anticipation. When a young woman of one hearth pulled out a sample of the mix and tested it, they watched every move with the earnestness only the young could portray. Their eyes were enormous in the darkness and some adults teased them for their greed. They petted their hair and patted their tummies to let them know dinner was on the way.

The young woman tasted and then shook her head. Not ready yet. The disappointed youngsters then stared at the slow tendrils of steam lifting from the pots, testing the air with eager noses to taste the smell of dinner.

The next person to test a pot was the speaker from earlier. She used a forked stick to reach into the pot and retrieve one of the stick bugs. This she removed from its casing and tested with a snapping bite that severed one half from the whole, which she chewed and swallowed. The children were rapt in watching each crunching of her jaws, swallowing in reflexive sympathy when she did. They leaned forward eagerly, each holding their own forked stick.

"We must wait," the older woman admonished. "We must feed the spirits before we take our own nourishment."

There were groans of despair when she fished out one of the precious crayfish and set it on a slab of bark. "We are not savages," she retorted. "The spirits have blessed us this night and we will thank them justly!" She then laid two stick bugs and four of the boiled tubers onto the trencher. This she walked toward the front of the cave and set on a boulder. I swear it was not my imagination that saw her step between Cernon and I, side-stepping two steps to miss me, then angling the other way to miss him. Could this one see us? What must we look like to her? Why did she not point us out to her tribe if so?

When she returned to the central fire, a quick signal had all the head women of each separate hearth drawing the meals from the steaming pots. First served were the gatherers. But the children were next and received generous portions. The adults reached in to gather the last of the meal with cupped palms when it had cooled enough, wasting not even that nutrition from the soup.

Once dinner was over, the head-woman stood and moved to the back wall. When she withdrew a red-ochre piece of rock from the bag she wore from her shoulder, the entire tribe moved to settle around her. She looked around the group, seeming to pause for a closer glance in our direction, then she turned to the wall. When she started drawing in swift, sure strokes, she amazed me at how quickly Cernon took form. Then I gasped when the artist depicted a fur-clad woman at his side. Apparently, both Cernon and I were to be immortalized in red-ochre lines.

The small antlers adorning the female's head caught me by surprise, though, and I reached up to my head, running a hand over it. I wondered if the transition into this place had included a new set of antlers.
The shaman woman laughed aloud when she saw my gesture yield no sprouting tines. Then she turned to embellish my figure further with ample breasts which I had never had, or wanted.

When she completed her drawing, she turned to the tribe. "Blessed we are on this night," she told her people. "The spirit of Deer is with us to guide us in our preparations for the coming hunt. We must set up a welcome for he and his companion that they will share their wisdom with us." She motioned with her hands and several of the young men stood to retrieve leather bags from a cave/tunnel opening at the back wall. From these, they withdrew many smaller furs which they laid out on the stone floor to form a sitting area. Next, they laid out collected antlers in a concentric circle, the butt of each discarded rack fitted into the top fork of the one before it.

The shaman stepped around the circuitous path, following the deer antler pattern, before settling down onto a pile of hides. Then she looked directly at Cernon and I, motioning us to follow the same path.

We obediently made our way into the conference area, and each of us took one of the seating pads. None of the others could see us, I realized. They kept their keen gazes on the shaman, even when we passed between her and the viewers. I noticed, though, that her eyes followed us hungrily as we rounded the circle to our places.

"They are with us," she intoned in a harsh, guttural whisper that had the impact of a shout from her rapidly lifted and spread arms, which ended up pointing directly at each of us.

The children drew into the protective embraces of their families, fearfully looking around for the phantasms. The younger adults were obviously fearful as well. They, though, practiced stoicism instead of allowing their apprehension to show.

"Tell us of the coming hunt," the shaman requested once we had settled.

I looked to Cernon, who seemed out of sorts sitting cross-legged on a pile of furs. He lifted a finger from the hand on his near knee, letting me know he was to be the spokesman for us.

"The deer are going to travel along a different valley," Cernon informed her. "The snow and ice have blocked their normal path. And they have diverted around the higher pass and into a valley further away. If you try to set your normal plan, you will go hungry for the season."

"I thank you for this information," the shaman said. "I, Gwyniffred, Vision-seeker for The People, honor your message." She looked away from Cernon, her eyes traveling around the assembled clan. "The hunt will be more difficult this season," she relayed. "The deer-great-one tells me that the heavy snows have filled the passes, and the migration will be along a different route, further from our home than before."

There were gasps from the assembled, and one grizzled hunter stood. "What evidence is there of this new migration path?" he asked. "If we change our plans and the deer use the same route as they always have, we will go hungry for an entire season. It will lose many of us to the great starve!"

Some of the clansfolk nodded or grunted their agreement to this fear.

"Is it not enough that your Vision-seeker tells you this?" the shaman asked them. "What good is it to have a visionary if you doubt her revelations?"

"You have always been right," the doubter conceded. "Yet you've never once encouraged us to stray from tradition before this. It seems reasonable that there should be some proof before we take this risk."

"There is danger in your pronouncement," the shaman said gravely. "If the deer-great-one gives us proof this time, which I don't know that he will, you will then demand proof before any future decision as well. Better that you send your shaman out into the wilderness on her own than to hobble her in this way." She stood as if to pack her things, turning toward the circuitous route out from the meeting place.

"Wait," Cernon said. He scanned the surrounding members, looking for some sign. Then his glance settled on one young man. "You," he said, pointing, "you seem able to perceive me. Step forward so you can join us."

The vision-seeker stopped as directed, watching Cernon's gaze travel across the members. Her eyes widened in shock as the young man stood as directed.

The targeted man, he could only be a couple years into fathering age, with a beard less substantial than the vision-seeker's sparse strands, looked to either side, seeing that everyone else was rapt on the shaman and had not seen Cernon's summons. When he stood from his place, he drew the startled glances of his peers.

"What are you doing?" one hissed in alarm. "Sit down before they punish you!"

"The great one summons me," the lad answered earnestly. "I can't ignore him." Then he stepped forward, drawing the attention of the entire tribe.

"What are you doing?" the doubter interjected. "Return to your place."

"The antlered one has summoned me into this council," the lad answered. "Will the Vision-seeker confirm this for me?" He looked at the shaman.

"I saw the great one summon him," the shaman said. "I'm surprised that Wainson has seen this. Vision-seekers are rare, and to have two in a tribe even rarer." She motioned to the young men who had set up the conference area. "Place another seat," she ordered.

"What trickery is this?" the doubter interjected. "Did you tell him to support you in this way? What is your goal?"

"Silence," an older, far more grizzled man said from the largest hearth area. "As chief, I will allow the vision-seeker her way. We can't afford to anger the gods. Have you forgotten the reason for the hunger-deaths of ten seasons ago? Do you not remember that there was a long snow then, too? Think how valuable this new knowledge could be. We could allow for new births if the gods blessed us with a new spirit guide."

Only then did I look around enough to realize the significance that there were no children younger than six seasons amongst the assembled tribe. I had noticed it before, but had not considered it alarming, assuming that they kept the young ones separate from the major group. But there were no young children. This highlighted the pain this group had been suffering. No children! How had they managed it? Had they separated themselves, man away from woman for the entire time? Had they, all gods forbid, slain their young rather than see them starve?

"Tell us what you saw, Wainson," the chief ordered as the young man sat himself on a pile of furs between myself and the shaman.

"When Gwyniffred drew the goddess," Wainson said, "the goddess reached up to her head to show that she had no antlers. That was when Gwyniffred laughed out loud. Then the goddess made as if to speak and the god raised a hand to silence her."

"Why did you not tell anyone what you saw?" the chief asked.

"I wasn't sure it was real," Wainson answered. "It seemed as if it were a waking dream and not something that was happening here, in our hearth place."

"This is true," Gwyniffred said. "Usually, when I see the gods, they seem very unfirm. As if they were misty images playing in the air. It seems I could brush my hand and erase the vision." She paused as if she were remembering her earliest views.

"What made you stand and come to the conference area?" she asked of the young man.

"The god sought me out," Wainson answered. "He looked all around the room and he captured my eye, calling my attention to him."

"Had you seen him before that?" Gwyniffred asked.

"I had seen shifting shadows as they moved," Wainson answered. "I thought them to be mere shadows from the flickering firelight, but each time they were moving, you were following them with your eyes."

The shaman looked at the chief. "It appears to be a genuine awakening," she said. "Can we ask for Nevrensor's silence while we continue this meeting? I wouldn't have him stifled. We value all input to keep our tribe strong, yet he interferes in this very important process with his baseless objections."

"The doubter will be silent," the chief ruled. "I will reserve the right to question Wainson in what he sees and hears. I will want to know what he thinks as well. If we're to have another prophet among us, we need to be assured that he sees true."

The chief looked at Nevrensor next. "I know you have doubts, Nevrensor. We all do. Yet, we have survived as a people because we've believed our prophets. Your background with the Genessee Tribe brings you to doubt because your tribe didn't have a vision-seeker and you've not seen the evidence of the Sight. When this event concludes, after the hunt, then we will re-visit your concerns. If," he added, "you still have concerns. For now, remain attentive to the conference and hold your objections for later consideration. And," he pointed at the doubter for emphasis, "remember that your clan is no more. The great hunger took them."

"As you command, Chief Agamon," Nevrensor said. "I will watch for treachery in silence."

Cernon startled at this last, reaching for his spear before subsiding.

"What did you see?" Agamon asked of Wainson. "I saw you flinch and your face has paled."

"The spirit reached for his spear when Nevrensor accused us of treachery," Wainson said. "His demeanor became stern and fearsome, but then I saw him control his anger and settle again."

Agamon looked at the shaman. "Is this true, Gwyniffred? Did the god become angered at Nevrensor's words?"

"Yes, Agamon. His mien showed anger. I think, though, that he is a good great-one because he stifled that anger instead of lashing out as if Nevrensor were a true enemy."

Nevrensor's widened eyes and flared nostrils showed alarm at the direction of the conversation. Even for someone who doubted the ability to see into the Other World, he seemed to realize it was unlikely that the two would have cooked up such a detailed set of observations. He looked as if he would say something, then saw the chief glaring at him and sat back in his place in the circle of tribe members.

Cernon showed Gwyniffred the layout of the new valley the deer would follow. He suggested how to best harvest the migrating deer. When she drew his plans out on the wall with her red ochre, many of the hunters recognized the valley. They agreed that, if the deer were to travel that path, Cernon's plan would be the best one.

Chapter Four

Reflections

Once the tribe had settled in for sleep, leaving fires banked against the cold, I felt free to quiz Cernon. "How long are we staying here?" I wondered. "It was afternoon when we started this journey and we've been well over twelve hours in this place."

"Humans always insist on time," Cernon answered. "I've told you, and Jamari, and many others before, that time is not the same in the Other Worlds. Especially here in the Middle World. We are meeting the ancestors. If you are to insist on 'time,' we are over fifty thousand years in the human past. Millenia before language or thoughts were ever written. In a time when early humans drew their thoughts and visions on walls, with many more millennia before they invented papyrus or paper. You are seeing the first of the followers of Cernon." He paused and looked around the sleeping tribesmen at their hearths, then looked at me again. "How tired do you feel?"

"Not tired at all," I answered. "I feel as if I could stay awake this whole night and still have more energy to burn."

"It has been just long enough for you to have blinked thrice in the Dream World," Cernon said.

I have to interject something here. The people of the Middle World refer to my "real" world as the "dream" world. They think of it that way because they believe they "dreamed" us into being, thus creating a living tapestry that has lasted for millions of years. I, however, know that my world is "real" and that the Middle World is the one where I go to "dream."

"Blinked three times," I parroted back to him. "When a full day has passed here."

"Fifty thousand years," I said again in awe. "It feels as if I'm really here. Not as if it's a shaman dream at all."

"Why would you think you are NOT really here?" Cernon asked. "Look at the picture on the wall. Is that not a likeness to you? Did not the Vision Seeker draw it while looking directly at us?"

"It's a lot to take in," I said defensively. "Time is immutable. We cannot escape it. We cannot control it. We certainly cannot travel it!"

"And yet here we are," Cernon answered.

We both turned to look at one hearth where a couple were engaging in eros, silently so as not to awake the others. I thought of the lack of children again and wondered if they were breaking taboo.

"It is two men," Cernon answered my unspoken thought. "The Elk Creek Tribe controlled their population during the fall of the western world by encouraging homosexuality. These people have reached a similar conclusion."

"Will the hunt tomorrow ease that restriction?" I wondered.

"It will," Cernon said. "And we'll be a part of that new burgeoning."

Startled, I looked at him in the flickering firelight. "You mean we'll be encouraging them?"

"You'll see on the morrow," Cernon said smugly.

My pondering that night drifted back to an earlier year with Jamari. Back to our exodus from Milltown Village and our move to the Founder's Grove.

***

Jamari knew, going into our seclusion on Milltown Hill, that Chief Matthew had been working against him. It was one reason we moved up to the Founder's Grove with our two miracle sons.

Evan was the first of them, he who was the first of the Children of Jamari. When we made him, under the influence of the Great Spirit on the day of awakening, we knew he would be special. Jamari and I still held each other, joined in eros, when we looked into each other's eyes with a shared knowing. We had known at that moment this son was going to be someone very special indeed. We knew this even as the God Force withdrew from us.

This "knowing" stayed with us even after we descended from the Upper World influences. As you'll know from prior sections of my memoirs, those of us who could travel to the Upper World often lost recollection of our experiences there. We could recall the sense of wonder; the general happenings. But we always "knew" that there had been more to our adventure than we could remember when we returned to the mundane.

Now, nearly eighty years after that day of miracles, I'm writing this section of my experiences.

Jamari is gone now, though that doesn't tell near enough about his current state. Which brings us back to one day in the Founder's Grove.

We had carried some few belongings up the hills with us as we abandoned our home in the village below. We had been certain that once Chief Matthew passed, or the tribe removed him, we would go back.

Don't misunderstand. We had the raw power (both influence amongst the tribe and favor from the Great Spirit) to take him down. Both of us recognized that spiritual leaders, while influential in the affairs of governance, should never use their influence to control it. Down that path lies tyranny!

Those were the days of our exile as I've written of before. What I need to tell of today is of another adventure, one so grand that it surely eclipses all of human experience gone before!

The tale of the battle of the Founder's Grove began Jamari awakened the Founder in his glade. And from the many tales of those who witnessed the awakening of the totem tree he had built. The salmon runs, which even today return to the base of that new tree to spawn, were created when his carving came to life and the Father and the Mother Salmon splashed down into the burbling stream.

Miraculous as they are, the salmon are the least of the new life that came into our world on that day! There are still reports that a great Roc inhabits the eyries of Hobart Butte, guarding the northern passage into our lands. Far too many witnesses tell of that great entity arising from the totem and shaking off the wooden exterior Jamari had carved. The tales of the horned men who guard Milltown Hill also are difficult to deny. In fact, the Tuatha Dé Cernon are the foundation of this tale I'm living and relaying now.

Jamari gained great power on that day. And those who already held power weren't ready to yield theirs.

Years before this event, the then-Knight Shaman, Terry, had been teaching Jamari about spirit-walking. Jamari discovered a heretofore unknown ability that day. He could separate his spirit from his body and still maintain enough cognizance of his body to animate both essences.

One day, a couple months before our exile, Jamari had been practicing this skill as he walked amongst a crowd of admirers. He was transiting the catacombs of Milltown Hall on the way to a tribal moot that Chief of Tribe Matthew had called. As he stepped into the great hall, his shadow spirit, which had been trailing along with the entourage, discerned a man pulling a knife from a hidden sheath. This man was behind Jamari and out of his physical knowing, but his spirit-self warned him.

With a suddenness that stunned the onlookers, Jamari spun his physical body around and grabbed the arm swinging the weapon toward his back. He twisted it such that it impaled the breast of the would-be assassin instead.

That man's eyes bulged in the shock and pain of it as Jamari pulled the knife from the assailant's chest. He wrenched it out of a dying hand and held it up toward the dais where Chief Matthew awaited Jamari's presence.

"It seems you've lost your knife," Jamari shouted over the sudden susurrus of dismay as those who witnessed the attack gasped out their amazement. The man thudded down onto the stone floor of the keep. "I see here the very knife I gifted you on the eve of Winter Tide two years back!" Jamari exclaimed loudly. "How comes it into the hand of an assassin?"

Chief Matthew made a great show of amazement as he reached down to his side and removed a knife from the sheath there. It was obviously a substitute, and all could see it. "He took it from me while I was walking through the crowds," Chief Matthew announced.

There was doubt whether even the slightest of touches could have unlatched the sheath and then substituted another knife without Matthew knowing. Yet the fiction was a way to avoid open conflict. The tribe suspected Matthew, from that day, of ill-intent, but none could imagine why the most powerful chief in the tribe's history would lash out against his Knight Shaman in such a way.

So many times, man has shown limited imagination when those who hold power refuse to share that power. Jamari was far too influential in the affairs of the tribe, and Matthew's plans were often subject to alterations from Jamari's suggestions and criticisms. No, those who hold power do not gladly share it. And Chief Matthew least of all.

At that point, our miracle son was only two and seemed content and able enough to thrive in the creche up in the women's hall at Elkhead. It was later when we realized Evan would become not just moody, but unruly and even dangerously violent, if we separated him too long from the touch of the wildwood. His ears, though obviously tipped as the elves of old, did not give us information enough to expect his needs as he grew. He needed the touch of the wildwood, to be in synch with the mycelium web.

It was this need, along with the continuing animosity from Chief Matthew, that brought us up to the Founder's Glade when Evan was six years old. Evan and his younger brother Rurick, then two years old. When we first arrived, Jamari used his power to cause the trees to form a sheltering arch, which we made into our retreat.

One day, Matthew, still not satisfied that he had curtailed Jamari's influence, sent a full cohort of trusted soldiers against us. He intended

Jamari should die in the glade. Instead, we survived, with a great deal of help from someone who had come into our world on the day of awakening.

Not Founder Knight, who you may suspect. No, this was Cernon. Or Cernunnos to some. Or Pan to others. High King of the Fae who came to live in the Founder's Glade. Who swore to protect the world from evil.

Cernon. The companion of my current adventure in journeying.

"Will I ever know what became of Jamari?" I wondered aloud in the middle of that long night while waiting for the tribe to awaken.

"Jamari's story has not ended," was all Cernon would tell me. And no amount of cajoling would coax a satisfactory answer from him.

Chapter Five

The Hunt

I must admit to having drifted off as the night wore on. Not that I slept. I felt no need for such. I did, however, travel far in my thoughts, thinking of my children and my choice to only allow Jamari to father them on me. Wondering at the youngest three, who were so very different from other children of their ages.

When this new tribe arose in the morning, the dawn was still far away. Each hearth had a designated attendant who awoke mid-way through the night to add fuel to the dying flames, but most slept the night through. Seemingly, it was the chill that awoke them as the fires had died down to the last dim coals. A new someone from each hearth then rose to tend the flames while the others rested quietly in their furs. As the cave brightened in the firelight, others arose from their slumber as well. The dawn was barely pinking the horizon when we all emerged from the cave to begin our march toward the distant canyon where Cernon had said the deer would arrive around noon.

Though some women were with us, including the Vision Seeker, most remained behind and we saw them setting up drying and smoking racks in anticipation of success as we rounded the river bend below and began our climb up and over the ridge.

We expected to be there with just enough time to set up our hunting zone before the predicted arrival of the migration.

I was hopeful on their behalf, as I saw many rubbing their aching bellies, which had seen no food since the scant morsels of the night before. As they traveled, I saw them stop to pull up a root occasionally. When they consumed the raw, wriggling worms they found, I realized I would probably perish of the hunger before I could hold down such a repast. They seemed energized from them, though.

When we descended from the last ridge and into the target valley, there were looks of concern from some. We had seen no sign of the deer. If they didn't arrive, this decision would be disastrous for the little tribe. They couldn't expect to survive on worms and grubs. Worn hides couldn't be replaced by woven grass. Not and still survive the extreme cold of this clime.

"Start setting up your stand here amongst this set of boulders," Cernon told Gwyniffred. "Have the men lay out their spears beside them and then we will wait."

Gwyniffred relayed the directions in their guttural language, which included the almost poetic visual arm and hand motions.

"There's nothing here," Nevrensor complained. "What folly is our 'vision seeker' playing at now?"

"Do as she says," Agamon ordered. "If our vision seeker is leading us astray, we have no hope for any future and we may as well perish as a tribe working together than to fall into strife and tear at one another as starving wolves."

There was a long time of wood clacking against wood as the group prepared their spears. Nervous hunters ran thumbs carefully along stone points to assure sharpness. One suffered a lacerated thumb which he put into his mouth to ease the sting.

Then was silence as we waited within the nest of boulders. The sun seemed at its peak through the dark clouds. There were birds coming back to life and singing of the spring as they forgot the intrusion of the group of humans. Even a bold vole danced across the feet of one hunter, making good its escape before he could scoop it up for a snack.

A loud snap sounded from down the stream. A broken limb. Then another. The men quickly picked up their spears and stood crouched behind the concealing boulders. The first of the herd to pass was a lone female, leading the way.

"Let her go by," Agamon ordered in the language of the hands without voice. "Let the leaders pass, then allow the rest to come to us undisturbed before we strike."

The hunters were shaking in eagerness as they watched the lead doe trot past them. She was close enough that they could see her withers shake off a pursuing nest of biting flies. We all caught her scent, rancid with sweat and the loam she had apparently rolled in at some earlier part of the day.

They allowed several others to pass, then when two young bulls passed to either side of us, Agamon lunged forward with his lance. "Take only young males," he said as he watched blood gush from the wound. The injured animal leapt to the side. Agamon held onto his spear. When it broke free from the skin, a more substantial wound opened and the animal plunged away in shock. He thrust out at another when he saw his spearpoint was still intact.

The deer seemed bereft of their senses as they continued to follow the path of their migration. The herd split around the nest of boulders where the hunters waited, trotting by, stepping over the bodies of their fallen brethren. There were so many that for several moments, the men only stared at the mass of trotting animals.

"Take only the ones you can get your best penetration on," Agamon ordered. He thrust his spear into the ribs of a stout bull as it trotted by. This animal lunged, breaking the shaft of the spear. There was just enough of the shaft buried inside that it became a channel for the heart's blood to flow out. The mortally injured buck spraddled his legs, leaning back onto his hind ones to take weight from his injured forequarters. He lifted his head, swiveling his eyes to lock onto Cernon as he passed into the next world, then fell at their feet.

Cernon's eyes shed water in recognition of the connection. Then he drew both arms inward, cradling and absorbing a ghostly spirit into himself.

Chaos reigned for the next few minutes as the men thrust their points into the sides and bellies of their targets. "Cease!" Gwyniffred then commanded, the only one not caught up in the blood lust. "We have more than we can use already, and we must honor the spirits of those we have taken."

"There will never be enough!" shouted Nevrensor. "How can you ask us to pass this opportunity by when we've been so long hungry?"

The hapless herd continued to stream past their hideout, dancing over the bodies of the fallen, churning the dirt into a bloody mass of thick, red mud. The rest of the men let their remaining spears fall slack in their grip as they gazed on the success of their hunt.

"It is not our way to slaughter what we can't tend," Gwyniffred answered.

"This is true," Chief Agamon said. "Cease your harvest!"

Nevrensor disobeyed and plunged his lance into the side of a fat-looking doe, twisting it so she could not escape and then he plunged his stone knife into her throat, letting loose a gushing of red blood and silencing her death bleat.

Then he looked down to see blood blossoming from his chest as Cernon plunged his knife into the man's heart.

"The god has killed him," one man shouted. "I saw the antlered one as he thrust!"

"Nevrensor has gotten what he deserved," Chief Agamon said. "We cannot survive as a people if we cannot work together. If we cannot escape the blood lust. We must honor the land, and especially the creatures that feed and clothe us. I, too, saw the god as he carried out this justice." Chief

Agamon bowed to where Cernon had been when he felled the dissenter, not seeing that Cernon had stepped away and was weeping into his hands.

"We will learn from our god," Agamon said, "and use his lessons to make us a better people."

I went to Cernon to comfort him, wondering at the grief.

"It is always thus," Cernon said, his voice shaking through his tears. "The deer sometimes recognize what is coming. That was bad enough, but then I had to fell Nevrensor. I can't abide the pain of taking a life, yet we must, in order to ensure the survival of the larger whole."

"Trail the injured deer who fled," Agamon told the remaining men, oblivious to the crying god. "Follow the blood trails and relieve them of their misery if they survive. Bless each one and thank them for their sacrifice, which feeds us."

He reached over one young bull, injured, lying on the ground beside the hunters' refuge of standing stones. The animal was trickling a runnel of frothing red from his muzzle, and Agamon thrust his knife into its throat. "Thank you for giving of your life that our tribe may survive," Agamon said as the light faded from the animal's eyes. "May your journey to the next life bring you joy." Then, he turned to watch that his men were doing as instructed.

Once the hunters had attended all the animals, the men eviscerated the dead, then peeled the warm hides away from the lax bodies. As the meat was cooling in the chill air, the hunters worked the hides into fresh forms. When they were done, the skins became bags used to carry the meat back to the cave.

When a pack of carrion dogs showed up to take their share, the men tossed odd scraps to them, letting the scraps guide the predators away from the main slaughter site.

As the afternoon wore on, the hunters donned packs filled with meat, leaving the bones behind. Though they staggered under the weight of their loads, they had to hang some meat in trees for a follow-up trip the next day.

It would be well past dark when we arrived at the cave, even at the fastest of paces.

Chapter Six

Celebration and Planting

The second night after the harvest, as skins were curing and meat was smoking over multiple fires outside the cave entrance, with an ample amount wrapped in clay for roasting in the coals, the tribe agreed to end the long prohibition on mating.

Agamon sent the oldest members of the tribe off to a separate cavern with they youngest. The rest of the breeding age adults shared meat and danced out pantomimes of the hunt, of the processing, and of the work the men and women did together to provide for the tribe. The dances became very amorous with this tribe, but not openly erotic until the right time.

Gwyniffred and Agamon together decided when it was time to begin choosing partners. First, though, both walked back toward the separate cavern to confirm that the youngest were asleep and safe under the care of the oldest.

When it was time to choose partners, I encouraged Gwyniffred to choose the much younger Wainson. I didn't even stop to think that what I was really doing was to encourage the vision-seekers to share genes in order to create a line more likely to produce others in the future.

When I stepped over to his place in the circle to invite him to the vision seeker's hearth, he showed shock. I wondered if he thought I was offering myself to him.

Impossible, I thought to myself. A misty union at best, I thought, with valuable seed spilled onto infertile stone. I smiled at him and held out my hand. When he rose, I saw evidence of his anticipation of the event. I led him to Gwyniffred.

He appeared in awe and fear of the opportunity to mate with the seeker, yet his arousal did not diminish.

The tribe had sealed off the cave to the night's cold. The smoke from the fires was trailing up and through natural chimneys, so we were all warm enough to shed some layers of furs. Cernon had stripped down to his customary bare skin. When Gwyniffred crouched onto her knees and lifted her remaining fur to expose her sex to Wainson, Cernon's manhood also rose. I watched in fascination as it lengthened, unhooding the head as it rose above his swaying purses.

"Will you share with us?" Gwyniffred asked, seeing Cernon's response.

Cernon looked at me, forwarding the question with hungry eyes. I had desired none but Jamari, yet could not deny this moment. I mimicked

Gwyniffred's position, crouching onto hands and knees, and lifting my remaining fur as well. Looking back, I saw Wainson move the pouch of his breech to the side, revealing his eager rise.

I moved closer to Gwyniffred when Cernon gestured me to do so. Had we been on the same plane, our hips would have been touching. She, though, moved even closer. Her physical body merged with my ephemeral one.

When Wainson knelt and placed his shaft against her opening, I felt its glistening heat myself. And I felt it as he rubbed the length of her opening, spreading their shared slickness until his tip probed into her depths. I shuddered with her at the slick heat of his entry. The quickening of his breath and hers matched as they became one.

Then Cernon knelt behind us all and placed his corona against Wainson's thrusting backside. Wainson gasped as Cernon's heat passed through him and into contact with me.

I felt the larger size he brought into play and wondered at the sensation. I had only ever felt Jamari in this way, and Jamari, while perfectly shaped, was far smaller than Cernon. When Cernon shifted his head so that it found the center of my opening, I felt his increasing moisture meeting with mine.

I turned my head around to the left and saw our shadows on the cave wall.

There, Wainson's shadow showed him thrusting into Gwyniffred, with my shadow superimposed over hers. Cernon's shadow also danced on the rock wall, poised for entry. It looked for all the world as if we four were a single joining. As in fact we were when Cernon gently slid his mass through Wainson and into my opening until I could feel his tightening sack against my lower lips.

Wainson gasped as Cernon slid his ethereal length through his physical body and those two became one as both males sought their release in the joined pair of Gwyn and I.

The joined males thrust into the joined females in driving need. We two females joined in our quivering acceptance. When I could feel Cernon reaching his highest point, he reached a rough hand down and gently opened my forward folds to expose my pleasure bud. As he groaned out his release, he pressed and rubbed on this point until Gwyniffred and I fell into a paroxysm of shuddering pleasure.

I could feel his throbbing as he released his seed into me, and I felt my body's response drawing that seed deeper into my core. I sensed that

Wainson, too, reached his extreme and felt his hot seed pulse into the Gwyniffred-Sophia pair. When the single male being of Cernon-Wainson completed His release, the single female being of Sophia-Gwyniffred felt the shrinking diminishment of their withdrawal. I could feel her emotional regret at that withdrawal. Matching my own.

We are one, I thought to myself and felt her agree.

For how long, I wondered.

Until we birth our babe, she answered. Was that hope I heard in her spirit-voice?

This was not an encouraging answer for me. Despite Cernon's assurances that time moved differently in this realm, a full cycle of gestation seemed far too long to be away from my body, in my time, at my home. I was thinking of time, even though he had assured me it was a human creation that we had trapped ourselves into.

Gwyniffred startled a wordless question at me. What is this 'time?' she wondered.

I quickly focused my thoughts on the present. Looking at the flickering wall shadows, I saw the shadow of the Wainson-Cernon entity separate from us. "The gods partnered with our vision seekers," one proclaimed. Then I heard the shocked awe from tribal members who had seen the shadowy coupling as well. All of them interrupted their own mating to see the shadow-picture-show, where Cernon stood and stepped back behind the fire to disappear from their perception. Wainson sagged down onto the sleeping furs in post-coital relaxation.

I couldn't deny it for Cernon, but I was sure that I was no god.

When I saw the horned form of Cernon separate from the physical form of Wainson, I realized it would spare Wainson an unexpected internal haunting.

Though, as I thought about it, that's not how I was seeing the joining with Gwyniffred and I. We were of a similar mind, with a similar goal: to birth this miracle that was surely growing within our joined self.
Would Wainson expect future couplings? I wondered. What would that be like? With Jamari and the restrictions of the Elk Creek Tribe, there had never been a coupling just for pleasure. Once I was pregnant, that was the end of the joining, and Jamari went back to the Men's Hall as I went off to the Women's. I looked over to where Wainson was tucking himself back inside his breech with curiosity.

If you want it, we can make it happen, Gwyniffred told me.

I'll think about it, I answered.

When I turned back to face the tribe, I saw other couplings concluding. I witnessed two couplings of male to male as well, since there were too few women to pair with all the men.

Our food-drugged bodies pulled us down and into sleep as the night descended. I wondered at my response as I drifted off. Did our joining mean I would have a more complete and real connection to this time and this tribe?

Regardless, there would be children in the tribe once again. If not from this first night, then from one of the many that were sure to follow.

Chapter Seven

Gestation

Will we reveal our oneness to the tribe? I wondered at Gwyniffred.

I think to the chief, she answered in our two-in-one-mind soliloquy mode.

This will take some getting used to, she thought to me.

Yes, I agreed. I've had conversations in my head before, but I've always known what each voice would say before they said it. You surprise me often.

We could take advantage of the situation, she said.

How's that?

We could exchange knowledge of the magic and how best to interpret what we find.

I think there's something better I could share with you, I realized.

What? she thought at me.

I'm a medicine woman, I told her, using the term we had long used to describe one such.

What is a medicine woman? she asked.

One who knows the healing properties of the plants, who understands the inner workings of the body and who can heal the sick and injured, I told her.

Ahh. That could be valuable, she agreed.

Besides, you're already very skilled in vision-seeking, I told her. And we can develop Wainson more in that role. So, since we'll have plenty of time, I'll teach you what I can.

Why don't I just suddenly know everything you know, Gwyniffred wondered.

I think, though we are two closely connected entities, I said, that's not equal to being the exact same entity.

Ahh, she said, seeming not to understand any better than I what this joining meant.

When I think a thought to you, you 'hear' it, I told her. If I don't think it, you can't perceive it.

Let's start with wound healing I suggested in some alarm as our glance passed over Chief Agamon, who was rubbing one hand over a reddened scratch I had been watching since the harvest. Do you see the redness around his cut?

Yes, she said. I have seen it before on others and it almost always goes away.

What happens if it doesn't, I asked her.

He'll die, she answered.

Then, let's get him aside and we can treat him as we also explain our joined existence.

"You have a cut going bad," Gwyniffred told Agamon as we approached.

He lifted his arm up to look at the cut. "It has been so many times before," he said, "and it always goes away."

"The goddess says that this one will only get worse and you could die," Gwyniffred answered.

"How is it that the goddess pays attention to one such as I?" he asked.

"We have become one," Gwyniffred told him. "When we joined for the mating, we stayed joined. I hear her thoughts and she hears mine."

"Why didn't Wainson stay joined with the deer-god, too?" Agamon asked.

"Cernon, the deer-god, separated from Wainson because Wainson wasn't ready for that level of joining yet, having just awakened into vision-seeking," we answered the chief.

I started some water heating in a bag as a prelude to treating his cut.

"Why are you cooking so early?" he asked. "It's only just mid-morning and dinner isn't until after dark this early in the year."

"We're going to be making a poultice to draw the poison from your wound," the pair of us answered. "We saw the redness from the other side of the cave and have seen how you are favoring it and rubbing it to soothe the ache."

He reached down to caress the swollen arm. We reached out to test the swollen area. "It's warm to the touch, too," we said. "You will sit at your furs while we treat it."

"Who orders this?" he asked, looking into Gwyniffred's eyes.

"Sophia is my name," I told him. "I apologize, Gwyniffred, for speaking out of turn instead of allowing you to carry the message more appropriately to your ways."

"It shows that there is another in her soul," the chief said. "Gwyniffred would never have given her chief a command. Even IF it were to save his life." Agamon held his arm out where I could examine it. It was overly warm to the touch. And swollen. My concern rocketed. This cut would have advanced into a full-on infection. Maybe still would. We needed to get the poultice going as soon as possible.

Do you know where there might be some chickweed emerging? I quiet-asked Gwyniffred as I gathered some blackened charcoal from the edges of our firepit.

I don't know that name, she answered.

In a flash of concentration, I relayed what chickweed looked, smelled, and felt like. It is a plant with short, yet thick leaves, I described to Gwyniffred. The stems are mostly forked and have a line of hairs down either side. The leaves are broad and full-looking, with a light green color as opposed to the darker green of evergreens, egg-shaped with a pointy tip. It needs to be the one with small, white flowers and NOT the one with reddish orange flowers. If you've ever tasted it, it feels cool on the tongue with a minty sensation and salty. It smells like mint but with a twisted pitch to it.

"Get some chickweed," Gwyniffred ordered a passing girl as she recognized what I was talking about. The name she used, along with their arm motions at various inflections, would have been unpronounceable in the language I was most familiar with.

"Wainson, get some of the bluish mud from the stream bank," I used Gwyniffred's voice and directed, since he had ventured over to the chief's firepit to see what the commotion was about. She provided the arm motions. "I saw it just downstream from where you found the crayfish the other day. It needs to be the clay-like stuff with a bluish tint, not the brown or red stuff. I'll need about a double handful. Get it from just above the waterline by lifting the moss to expose the mud you'll be looking for. That will have the best drawing qualities."

When the others were going about their tasks, Chief Agamon looked at Gwyn and me again. "It will be difficult to maintain discipline if we don't tell the people what has happened. Is there any reason they should not know?"

I looked across the fire to where Cernon had been sitting. He seemed introspective ever since the hunt, and hadn't spoken all morning. "Cernon?" I asked.

He looked up from his contemplations. "Yes?" he asked.

"The chief thinks we'll need to tell the others that my spirit has joined hers in her body for a while because we aren't able to disguise my influence and it is going to break the hierarchy."

"Yes, it most certainly will," Cernon said. "They have seen enough now to know that the spirits are with them. I can't see any harm in telling them that one is 'visiting' in Gwyniffred's body for a few months. Just don't tell them about where we came from before being here. That's not something they'll be ready for until many generations have passed."

Gwyn looked shocked as we relayed this request. "Then, where ARE you from?" she asked.

"Another place is all I can say," I answered for us as Cernon looked alarmed. "There is real danger in asking too much about this. It is a god-thing." Cernon shuddered at the description, yet held his peace and let the statement stand.

Gwyniffred seemed to go digging in our shared mind-space for a better answer. As she picked at the concept of "time" in my thoughts, I felt genuine fear for her and her people. This small group was not ready for such a philosophical, and trapping, revelation. She sensed my fear even as she felt her own at the concept of years beyond counting unrolling in her mind.

I will leave it alone, she said in our shared mind. It seems you should have as well. Nor will I share this contamination with my tribe.

What could I say to that accusation? How many eons before my time had humankind fallen into that trap?

While we were waiting for Wainson to bring the clay, I used some of the now-hot water to cleanse the chief's wound. "How did you get this?" I asked the chief.

"There was a piece of spear point in one of the deer I was gutting," he said. "When I was pulling out the entrails, it cut me."

"There will have been deer's blood inside your cut," I said with alarm.

"The chief has the blood of the deer flowing in him!" an onlooker announced to those still in the cave, watching the process.

"No…" I opened our mouth to object, but Cernon held out his hand to silence me.

"It will be good for them to believe their chief has special connections," Cernon said. "They are too small a group to survive too many more deaths should anyone else decide to challenge him." Though still there, his sadness seemed to have given way to resolution.

We need to learn that not all my thoughts should be spoken, I told Gwyn.

I set to pounding the charcoal into fine dust after cleaning the wound. When Wainson brought back the blue mud, I mixed it with the charcoal and made a paste with hot water. Then I put that paste directly over the chief's wound and wrapped it in skins. "We need to wait for the sun to settle one hand's width," I said, "before the next step."

I had one of the younger women grind the chickweed in a pestle with some warm water and dandelion leaves.

Once the hour had passed, I removed the compress and carefully peeled the poultice away. Everyone could see the evidence that the concoction had drawn poisons from the chief's arm. The lip of the wound had whitened, and the poultice held a greenish-yellow pus. When I slathered on the chickweed and dandelion paste, he let out an "Oh" of relief as the mix soothed his pain.

"This will need to stay in place until the evening," I said. "Then we'll have to make another application."

The chief motioned all the tribe members over to the vision-seeker's hearth. "We have a miracle," he told them. "You've obviously noticed that Gwyniffred is behaving unusually. When the spirit one visited us three suns ago, he brought another spirit with him. Both are still with us to help us through our bad time. The woman-spirit is living within Gwyniffred so she can teach her the ways of the vision-seeker, as well as those of a medicine woman."

He paused and looked at Wainson. "Wainson will join Gwyniffred's hearth. She can take him as mate, or she can choose to use his services as she may. In either event, he too will learn from the presence of the spirit-woman. He has seen the god and can talk to him if needed."

Chief Agamon looked at Gwyniffred/Sophia again. "How will you take Wainson?" he asked. "Will he be a mate, or will he be a servant?"

My careless thought of that first night of breeding came back to me and we blushed. "We will take him as mate," we said.

Then, "I will still accept him as mate once the spirit-woman has departed," Gwyniffred added. "Will you accept us as mates?" She asked Wainson. "You are yet young and could find a younger partner if you so choose."

"I will take the path of the Vision-Seeker and be partner," Wainson said. "If I should find I need some younger lover, I reserve that right."

"Granted," the pair of us answered gladly. Neither of us wanted to tie him into a lifelong commitment with an older woman with only another eight or nine years of life left in her.

I discovered in this train-of-thought exchange that any of them living past thirty was a miracle and that Gwyniffred was already twenty-two and well past normal pairing age. Wainson was the perfect age, having passed puberty during the starvation time and maybe a couple years past prime mating age now.

We will work to extend those days, I vowed to my spirit-sister. As you learn to cleanse and value of cooking, you will get another eight or nine years at least.

Gwyniffred projected thanks at me as she motioned Wainson to her side and they/we held hands as they/we stepped over the fire together, joining us into a single hearth.

I had never been married before and this was a whole novel sensation to me. In my time and place, the community exiled "breeders," as those who married as heterosexual couples were called, to the fringes of the towns. I remembered my disdain/longing for that exact situation in my early years when I was so infatuated with Jamari. Gwyniffred projected questions at me even as we arranged the blanket hides for an added body. It's a whole new dynamic in a faraway tribe, I thought at her.

The chief flexed his arm in its wrapping, then motioned the rest of the tribe to give us space to settle into our new relationship. Gwyn seemed to wait for something as we arranged and then sat on the blankets. Wainson sat on them with us. We all wondered at the next steps.
He should give the signal to mate if he wants to complete the pairing, she thought at me.

I think he won't give you the signal, I told her. You've been the unreachable vision-seeker for too long and he isn't sure yet that his position is to be dominant in your/our relationship.

Gwyniffred nodded our head to this observation. "You'll need to accept your role as male/mate," she told Wainson. "It has always been the male who starts a mating."
We could see his breech pouch rise with his interest, yet he still seemed hesitant. I thought of just how young he was and remembered the careful lessons given in the Elk Creek Tribe before ever being expected to take part in breeding activities.

"We can make an exception for our first bonding," I offered. "Will you accept our touch?"

"Yes," he husked. He startled when I reached a hand down to caress his rise, then I deftly lifted the pouch to the side to reveal his manhood. They did not know of circumcision, I knew. An uncut male would be a novel experience for me, since they cut all Elk Creek men within days of birth. Gwyn lifted our hides to the side, and we settled into position on our knees, bottom in the air. Wainson had no difficulty with the next steps and

I enjoyed the quick entry and rapid thrusts until he seized us in rapt arms and shuddered himself into a deep, throbbing thrust.

He let his upper body come to rest on us as he settled from the sudden finish, his manhood still wetly embedded inside.

I thought it would be over, but then he pulled and thrust again, this time slower, and more carefully. Apparently, he had been paying more attention to Cernon's actions on that first night's mating than we had known, for he reached his hand around our hips to rub against our pubic hair, feeling for the fold which protected our woman's bud. When he teased those folds apart, we rocked in his grasp and Gwyn/Sophia moaned aloud our pleasure.

Wainson made his grip sure and then set to rocking into us again. He still maintained the slower, less frenetic, pumping, but he did it with determination, leaning his upper body onto our back, holding us tight in his arms. When his finger slid down the bud and into our wet folds, our excitement increased as the now-wetted finger came back up to caress the bud.

The joined pair of us near-howled our pleasure as he thrust up against us one more time and I/we felt his juices releasing into us again.

This time, he fell over and onto his back when he was done, panting out his pleasure. His wet manhood re-hooded itself as it retracted, his purses settling their tired prizes back down to a soft rest against his thighs.
We settled down beside him and pulled our hide blankets over all of us. We cradled him as he fell into slumber.

Chapter Eight

Time passages

Over that long summer and fall, Cernon and I taught the tribe how to better survive in a world that had been slowly cooling around them for generations. Many tribes had already fallen into extinction exactly the same as Nevrensor's had done. We made sure that our little group would not, and even took great pleasure in absorbing a lost family into the tribe when they wandered up the stream into our midst.

What is this 'genetics' you keep thinking of? Gwyniffred asked as we watched Wainson connect with one of the new women.

It was a moment of reflection for me. How to convey the danger of breeding too close to one's hearth? How to convince a people who did not know the dangers to avoid the results of such a practice?

I ran through a series of images in my mind, of deformed animals I had seen. She agreed they had seen such in earlier days.

It's a danger of breeding too close to your own family, I answered her finally. My people recognized this danger when we saw that animals who reproduced with their direct kin produced defectives far more often than those who instinctively avoided such crosses. We built a survival code, a taboo that was so deeply embedded that most members couldn't even think of violating it.

Perhaps we should consider it, Gwyn answered me in our thought-talk. We have witnessed abominations in the tribe, long before our starve time. They went away when we joined with another tribe. I never considered why. Now I have something to share with Chief Agamon.

We welcomed the newcomers: a couple of youngsters under six; three male teens just entering breeding age; the one woman Wainson had already mated; and several oldsters. In their old way, the tribe would have slain the men and taken the women as concubine and slave. Our group was amenable to absorbing them into their midst, so long as the men agreed to learn and practice our ways. None of us would ever forget the lesson of Nevrensor.

I taught Gwyniffred and Wainson the properties of many of the plants that prospered in the quick summer and even found one that when rubbed on our skin worked to repel the biting flies which were far more prevalent than I had ever suspected they could be from my far-future times.

We showed the women how to gather the seeds of the more proliferate grasses and then showed them how to make a rudimentary bread to supplement the meat that had been their main staple. With this added knowledge, and after showing them some careful testing methods to test new plant varieties for safety, they wouldn't have to suffer another starving time as they had before we came to them. We were teaching them to survive without us because we knew we would need to return to our own time soon.

In the fall, after preserving the hides from the spring harvest in a new way, and after learning how to smoke the meat and pack it so it would last for many seasons, we conducted a fall harvest of the south-bound return migration. We gathered in more meat for the long winter to come than the tribe had ever managed before. When we saw the salmon dancing up the falls, we added net making into their set of skills, then showed them how to smoke the orange flesh of the salmon as well. Cernon and I would not allow this tribe to see starvation again.

Many of the women were heavy with child by that time, though still a couple months away from birthing. Those who felt able went out with the gathering and hunting parties. The others stayed behind at the cave, preparing the fire and smoking pits for the coming harvest.

The men returned with full packs and, just as in the spring, had to set out again to retrieve that which they couldn't carry on a first trip. When they returned late that night, there was warm food for them and a celebration of survival followed. Any women who hadn't already been carrying surely would be soon.

Shorter days were ushering in the new season, and that night brought the first dusting of snow. The women who were pregnant were unavailable for a repeat of the spring celebration, so Cernon suggested a play wherein the hunters relayed in pantomime how they had conquered their prey. The suggestion reminded me of the shadow-show when our foursome joining had shown on the cave wall from the bright flames of Gwyniffred's hearth fire. Some experimented with that topic as a moving picture show to entertain the tribe.

There was great merriment as they experimented with the new medium. The "actors" settled themselves on hands and knees between the fire and the wall and joined in male partnering, strengthening the tribal bond. The shared Gwyniffred/Sophia body, aged as it was, had passed the point of sharing this pleasure with Wainson but he had found a willing partner in one man from the newly arrived tribe and those two set up their hide blankets separate from ours for their own bonding.

Winter Tide

I told Gwyniffred of the Winter Tide celebrations of my home tribe and she thought it would be a great thing to build up to as the season neared the shortest day and longest night. She was rapt as I relayed the story of Jamari's second time leading the Elk Creek Tribe in welcoming the Winter Tide season. Story telling was so easy when sharing details without laboring for just the right word or sentence to convey the thought. I wished our shared mind-talk could become a regular thing for all humans. Why could we not somehow make that happen? Gwyn asked.

We didn't have the capacity as a species, I answered. Instead, I sent her mental pictures and word-thoughts to describe a Winter Tide celebration.

***

Jamari was resplendent in his pale, almost white, deerskin leathers when he marched into the main cavern at Milltown Hall. He was glorious, with dark blond locks just beginning to cover his eyes as his hair grew out from his young-man days, when all those who took part in the Manhood Rites had their scalps shorn short. His blue eyes danced in the electric lights of the underground haven and his young calves bounced his lithe body up on tiptoes with every step as he made his way between the tables toward the main fireplace. He would light the waiting logs in that immense tower of mortared stone to begin the midwinter ceremony. He seemed completely unaware of how these prancing steps made him beautiful, bunching up his ass, lifting each side into a balled mass which swayed side to side as he strolled up to the front hearth.

There, the tribe's most recently retired Sophia Shaman, Lillian, awaited him alongside the previous Knight Shaman, Rodney. These two were to hold the honor of representing the ancestors in the coming ritual. Jamari swung himself around to face the hall as he reached the fireplace, causing the hind feed of his cougar-skin cape to swirl out and then settle in a slow swoosh to his feet.

"Welcome to Winter Tide," he sang out to the crowded hall. "Now is the time when the days are shortest, when the veil between life and afterlife are thinnest. We thank the ancestors for their role in coming safely through their times and giving us a world we can improve upon in our own way in our own time. Give them a moment of your thoughts as we prepare to welcome in the new Tide."

The lights dimmed at his words, leaving the hall in barely lit darkness with only a few far-off fireplaces lighting the background. "Ancestors of the Elk Creek Tribe," Jamari called gently, "we honor you in this time and ask that you watch over us as we pass through the straights into a fresh year. Counsel us as you can in dreams and visions as the veil weakens. And, should any of us pass through the veil to join you, please welcome us into your midst so that our tribe can celebrate them in their time."

Eyes adjusted to the dimness, and we could see rustling movement near the front of the room. Then we saw the prior Sophia Shaman kneeling at the fireplace, holding up a kindling laden board for Rodney Shaman. Rodney scraped a flint along a steel, creating a shower of sparks which he directed onto the tinder. When no sparks caught on that first try, he scraped out a tower of sparks again.

Lillian leaned down and puckered her cheeks, gently blowing a puff of air onto one spark which flared up in a tentative flame. She continued to breathe life into this tiny tendril as Rodney took up a splinter to feed the flame. When the splinter caught, he placed it further under the small mass of shavings. As the two worked the dry pile into a sustained flame, their shadows cast out from the front of the room, dancing in eerie rhythm onto the ceiling above as well as indistinctly onto the far back wall.

***

I had to stop my tale at several points to help Gwyn understand some concepts that simply weren't possible in her "now."

How there could be lights when the outside was dark. When she couldn't understand, I settled with the axiom we often landed at. "It's a god thing, from a far-off place." I enjoyed teaching her about tallow candles, though, and we later made some of those to the delight of the tribe.

***

When they set the kindled pile under the prepared sticks in the fireplace, the whole gradually caught and bathed the front of the hall in gently undulating orange and yellow flickers. Then, once the main logs had kindled, they stepped back to gaze upon the miracle of life brought into the cold stone fireplace which had been idly awaiting the re-kindling of the annual Winter Tide Fire.

Jamari stepped forward then, holding a long splinter into the flame. When this match flared to life, he stepped back and, cupping the small, dancing flame in his other hand, he carried the light over to the head table, where he lighted the first of the candles. Attendants carried these candles to the nearest tables. There, they were used to kindle the lights of those tables. They used the newly lit candles in their turn to bring light to the next until, in a chain of awakening, candles were alight all the way to the back of the room.

44

"As darkness takes sway over the land," Jamari said as the last tables' candles were being lit, we remember that these dark days will pass. We hold to our light as hope, and the comfort of our loved ones as we endure the season. We hold our cherished elders close as they contemplate their own passing through the veil as we honor those who have passed through. And we honor those elders who remain." He turned to his left and motioned with an upraised hand.

In a darkened corner, a young boy, still in treble voice, broke out in song. He greeted the ancestors in soaring notes, welcoming them into the company of the living. As he finished the first verse of his song, one that had raised the hairs on many a head in awe, a full choir joined him as they celebrated the season.

As the choir moved from one song to another, tribal members carried plates to the back tables where assigned young men and women set up the many dishes for feasting. There was salmon, freshly caught from the annual returns up Elk Creek. Roast elk, deer, and even fowl for those who wished it graced the table. The cooks had gone to their highest efforts to adorn the dishes with spices, and there was a tempting array of vegetable dishes as well. There would be no one leaving the banquet hungry.

At the shaman's table, the attendants brought two enormous platters for the shamans to choose their meals from. First, though, Jamari selected the finest cuts and dishes into a generous plate, which he sat at a lone table to the side of the hearth.

"Though our ancestors can no longer enjoy the simple pleasure of food well and masterfully cooked," Jamari said, "we give them of our best, anyway. Let their spirit feast, even if their bodies can no longer do so."

Many of the attendees glanced around the room as if expecting something more. Most remembered the first time that Jamari Shaman had performed the Winter Tide opening ceremony and the spirit of Bobcat had come into the hall to accept the offering. When it became apparent that Bobcat would not repeat the earlier boon, the attendees turned to their food, settling back at their tables, and taking up their utensils.

Chapter Nine

Gwyniffred and Sophia

I awoke from a dream one morning and realized that Gwyn was already awake. The dream had been stunningly real. My spirit remembered and honored my long-past relationship with Elena and I was near to tears with the memories it awakened in me. Gwyn and I's shared body was responding to the cues those old lessons Elena taught me had so often triggered.

Such a beautiful woman, Gwyniffred said to me in our two-minds-one-self language. Who is she?

I quietly wondered how many of my dreams she had been listening in on. Did I dare ask her?

That was Elena, I told her. She was my life partner for many seasons. She taught me the way of the woman and gave me her love before I ever knew what love could be. I'm ashamed at how long it took for me to realize just how much I really loved her.

Tell me more, Gwyn said as we shrugged ourselves tighter under the blankets against the cool of the pre-dawn air in the cave.

We had a system where young people who were ready to become adults in the tribe identified themselves as ready to face that life by taking on the challenges of the adulthood rites, I told her. In thought flashes of memory and explanation, I told her of the Womanhood Rites and the Manhood Rites. I told her how Elena had been my assigned mentor, tasked with teaching me the Night Studies and Women's Mysteries.

Why would women need a unique set of rites? Gwyn asked. What would be the harm in including both men and women in one set of instruction?

Many. And none at all, I replied in a very Cernon-like answer. Our bodies are very different in how they respond to sexual stimulation, I told her in a brief answer, which obviously needed more explanation in the coming days.

She laughed aloud in my head. Show me the lesson she was teaching you in this dream, Gwyn said. I want to know what has my body so awakened despite being swollen like a fat doe.

The Night Studies, I said. That was the group of lessons taught to the young in order to assure that they would give as well as receive pleasure as a part of eros. In my dream this morning, Elena was teaching me the joys of touch. On that long ago lesson, she kept both hands on my body, tickling, tugging, prodding, teasing, and then would apply her lips as well to bring me to the heights of pleasure.

Could not a man do that? Gwyn wondered.

Most of them don't possess the stamina, I said. Think about our couplings with Wainson. He learned a precious lesson from Cernon that first night and has used it to our pleasure each time after. But he only has that one spear in his quiver. Then, once he satisfies himself, he falls off to somnolence. It's a very man-like response, dating farther back than we can know.

But women? she asked me.

Yes, women, I answered. We have the stamina. We possess the level of care that makes us want to please. We know our own bodies and so we know those of any other women we set out to pleasure.

I felt our body flush and recognized it as desire. Perfectly normal in any woman going through pregnancy. Hormones raging through a normally calm body, heat rising to untenable levels.

Let's show you some techniques, I said to her. Those can become something you hold of me besides those of Medicine Woman. Then, when Cernon and I are gone, you can teach the other women as well.

She responded to the touches I gave her when I took control of her body. Try not to listen to my mind, I said. The surprise of each subsequent action is part of the pleasure.

She was gasping out her release in no time, and we settled back into our blankets. Pleasuring a body not yours, but one you have full sensation from, is a far easier task than the old dead-head way I knew with all my previous lovers. I could feel her response to each new touch, and felt the quickening of her breath, too. I knew precisely when to apply the best pressures.

When we were replete, we could pay attention to other activity in the cavern. Did our activities wake Wainson and the young man he had taken to his bed, or were they just now rousing to pleasure each other?

Why can't we teach the men to pleasure us? Gwyn asked again.

We can, I told her. And we have many times. Some are genuinely interested and they are the sought after partners. Others will give us that pleasure in order to get pleasure from us in their turn. But the tit-for-tat nature of that turns us away from pleasure. Most simply don't understand us, or our bodies, enough to help us. The biggest danger of all, though, is the possibility of unmanning them. If our demands are too much for their spirits, they can lose the ability to give us their seed. It is a careful path we must tread in order to pair with one of them.

Gwyn pondered my words and the thought-flashes that accompanied them. I love you, soul-sister, she said to me as we heard Wainson and his partner gasping out their release. I look forward to many more nights of learning the Night Studies from you.

Me too, you, I said to her. We will spend some time teaching the other women while I'm still with you, too. There is a word in my language that has so much negative connotation to it, that I almost don't dare use it. But it describes so well the dance we must enter with our men. Manipulation. Recognizing their weakness, we must encourage and help them perform without ever letting them know what we're doing. They do so need to be the dominant force and we must always act as if it's true.

Chapter Ten

Cernonson

The labor was sudden, early, unexpected, and severe enough to wake Gwyniffred/Me up from a sound sleep. When we cried out our alarm, Wainson rolled over to us from the blanket he now shared with his special lover from the out-tribe who was now a part of our hearth. Our little tribe was growing from without as well as from within as our women continued to swell.

"What is it?" he asked in alarm.

"Labor," I gasped as the contraction eased. "It's too early, though."

What does it mean? Gwyniffred asked me in our head.

I don't know, I answered back. I don't feel our body pushing, but that was definitely the drive to put out a babe.

"It's time for the two of you to separate," Cernon told us as he appeared at our head. "Your spirit-baby is to be born separate from your physical one."

"What?" the Gwyniffred/Sophia pair gasped out.

"Hurry," Cernon said. "If you don't separate in time, it will cause a sympathetic labor in Gwyniffred's body."

"How," I asked in confusion. "I don't even know how we joined in the first place."

"Think of how you can spare Gwyniffred the pain," Cernon said. "All you have to do is separate from her and she'll not experience the throes of birth until it is her time."

"But it's not MY time either," I moaned as another rippling pain shuddered up and down my abdomen.

"GET OUT!" Gwyniffred ordered.

And that was the key. The woman whose body had hosted my spirit for several months wanted me out and I was suddenly out.

I was bereft.

Alone.

No one to think a random thought to. No one to wonder a thought to me as she so often did. I looked down on her still supine body under the blanket and saw her eyes widen at the shock of separation as well.

"Alone," she whispered. "Just as I always was before, only now I feel the pain of it. Alone."

Our hearth fire flared up as Wainson added some fuel and stirred the coals to life. I could see a sudden welling of tears running down her face as she faced her new reality.

"I'll still be here for you," I said, reaching a spirit hand down to caress her face.

Then another rippling shudder crippled me down onto all fours. Apparently, a spirit body could still experience the upheaval of pain and discomfort. Who knew?

Once I was on my knees, I could feel the push of a babe. Exactly as I had experienced before when birthing Jamari's children. I pulled my knees forward, pushed my upper body higher, then squatted as a final paroxysm encompassed me.

When I felt a mass fall away, I turned to see Cernon cradling a furry little babe. Then I saw a baby human hand clutch Cernon's finger and a baby human face called out its fear at entering the world. He, and it was plainly a "he" with an out thrust pene, and tiny little purses which were as clear of hair as a human babe. His legs, though, had fur in a dark russet red, ending in tiny little hooves. When Cernon rolled him over, I saw a stub of a tail and fur running in a line up his bare little back. I reached for him and saw a reddening set of patches swell on his forehead. Then a set of tiny antlers prodded their way out and our son was whole.

"I think 'Cernonson' should be his name," Gwyniffred offered as she looked adoringly at the baby stag.

"It was always going to be," Cernon agreed. He handed him over to me to hold. "You'll want to hold him tightly while you can," Cernon said. "He's destined to grow quickly and will be full-sized before you know it."

I held the tiny miracle in my hands and he looked up at me from deep brown eyes, which were already filled with knowing compassion. This was a strong spirit force we had brought into being. Little Cernonson smiled at me, then reached his head forward, nudging inside my top to take in a nipple. I shuddered with the pleasure of it, having thought my days of child-bearing long past. "Should I cover him against the cold?" I wondered. "Does a spirit child even feel it?"

"He is spirit to this world," Cernon said. "Though he would feel the cold in ours, he doesn't feel it here. I'm sure he'll appreciate the closeness of a shared jerkin, though."

I pulled my new babe into the folds of my furs and relished the feel of his lips suckling life from my bosom.

Chapter Eleven

Going home

Cernon was true to his word on Cernonson's growth. The babe was terrible-two's in a week and was child sized in a month. After two months, he was thriving, young… well, what to call him? Man? Not really. With raking antlers which grew from his crown and the magnificent fur covering his legs and backside? With almost-elven ears, which he could swivel when he wanted to isolate the source of a new sound. No, not a young man, but a young spirit who bonded with his tribe.
It amazed me he seemed to hold knowledge that only Cernon could have.

"It is his nature," Cernon said. "You and I must return to our 'real' world. Cernonson will stay behind to guide his new tribe."

"You told me when we started this journey that I would see your beginning," I said. "Is Cernonson that beginning? Is he you, and are you he?"

"Yes," Cernon said. "That, and more. As he takes on the mantle of his position, he'll become more and more assertive. Eventually, we'll have to leave because there won't be room for us in his relationship with his people." He paused, apparently struggling to recall a time long past. "That is how I remember it, anyway."

That time came upon us before Gwyniffred entered her labor. All the women were reaching their times, and I was becoming fussy, trying hard to make sure they did nothing to harm the little ones they so desperately needed.

"You can't coddle them!" Cernonson shouted at me one day in a breaking voice which showed his advancement into early manhood. "This is not the Elk Creek Tribe. They haven't been through the thousands of years of softening that life subjected your people to. These babes will be born on rocky ground, then their mothers will set them aside while they continue to gather the food needed for the oncoming seasons. They will lay quietly under a bush until their mothers come for them in the evening. They'll eat dirt and roll in fundament, then wash it off haphazardly in the chill river water before rolling around in the dirt to dry. These women can't be coddled, and mothered, and cosseted as you want to do."

"You're right, Cernonson," I admitted. "I had hoped to stay for Gwyniffred's birthing, but I can see that my ways are causing my new people stress and confusion."

I looked for Cernon and saw him shadowing Wainson where he was coaching some men in the use of the atlatl Cernon had convinced Cernonson they would need to keep the tribe fed in the coming years.

We couldn't tell the tribe all the details, but we knew that the extreme cold was because of the encroaching glaciers and that this world would enter a long ice-age that would drive, or exterminate, humans from the northern climes. We hoped to give our tribe enough knowledge to survive, and even to excel as they had been doing since we had entered their world.

"It may be time for us to return to our own world," I told Cernon. "I've relayed as much as I can via spirit-talk with Gwyniffred and Wainson. Cernonson seems well in charge, and able to care for his people. I suspect we have reached the point where we are more hindrance than aid."

Cernon, who had overheard the entire fracas, looked to where Cernonson watched the women of the tribe flailing the seeds from some grass stalks. "I remembered him being willful at about this stage," he said. "It is time for us to let this quickening of mankind bubble into a yeast."

When it came time for us to depart, Cernon gave the tribe one last miracle. All their blades were stone and Cernon had carried an iron one in his sheath from when we came through the portal. He willed himself visible to the clan one last time and stood in all his glory as the tribe members beheld and honored him. Then he reached down to his side and removed the blade from its sheath.

"Agamon, I give this into your keeping until Gwyniffred's boy-child is of age. He is to have it as a symbol of his connection to me."

Cernon glanced to where Cernonson, now a strapping young man, stood at the back of the crowd. "You, Cernonson, will be the spirit-guide to these people. I have given you knowledge that you can use to aid them in surviving the coming challenges. You, having shared conception and a womb with that child, will communicate with him directly."

Cernon stepped forward and handed the blade, hilt first, to Agamon. "With this blade, you are the chief until the next one shall come and take it from your dead body," Cernon said. "For this first succession, knowing what we do about Gwyniffred's child, he will be fore-ordained to take the mantle. In the future, though the temptation will be strong to pass the leadership from father to son and so on down the line, I direct you instead to pass it to the one most able to lead. You, and every chief to follow, are to be assisted by a council you will form."

"I accept this burden," Agamon said, looking down with awe at the shining blade he held in his hands. "It's so light compared to the stone," he said, testing its weight and balance.

Cernon unlatched his belt, letting his clout fall to the ground. Nudeness was a very common occurrence in their tight-knit group, and I could tell that he was readying himself to return to our own time and space with that gesture.

Then he stepped to the chief and wrapped the belt with the sheath around his waist. Agamon slid the blade into its pouch, then knelt at Cernon's feet. "Thank you, Cernon, for saving our people. We will never forget what you have done for us and we pledge to honor your memory for all time."

Cernon reached his hand to grasp mine, and he carried us back into the kaleidoscope of the portal. No good byes. No time to share a lost thought with my spirit-sister. I had only the time to see her eyes widen as she watched the maelstrom form around us.

He had let them see the coruscant energy take us in as a part of the legend he wanted to build. Again, I had to cling to the essence of Him as the world dissolved around me and I dissolved into the mists of transition.

I gasped and collapsed to the ground again when we emerged from the transfer into a sunny afternoon in the Founder's Glade.

When I had caught my breath, I ran my hands over my body, re-familiarizing myself with it. What had been eight months in that other world had been only an instant in this reality. I wasn't even hungry and the slanting sun hadn't even marked me where it had been shining on my skin.

"How can I have so little sense of time passing?" I wondered.

"You always seem to latch onto time as a constant," Cernon answered. "It is as variable as any other element of the universe. It is only humans who have held onto the notion of a 'timeline.' The rest of the sentients in the multiverse can use it as they will."

"It still feels as if I lived that dream for real," I insisted. "How did Cernonson lead his people? What did Gwyniffred name her son? How did they move from where-ever it is that they were and to this continent, as I know they must have done? So many questions that demand their answers."

"You were never really there," Cernon assured me, evading the fundamental questions. "I took you through the veil, but only into the area where I placed my memories in the network. I built you a simulacrum body you could feel while you were remembering with me. You were riding my memories of a time so far in the past that I had forgotten it."

Chapter Twelve

Extrapolated Explanations

***

Now, as I write this memory down, I realize the immenseness of what he shared with me that day. He says he's not a god. He says it was only a memory he shared with me. Cernon, the father of the Tuath Dé Cernon in America. He is far more real to me now than he ever was before.

Avatar of Cernunnos, some have said. But, is that only because we can't envision what it is to stand on the same ground as a god? Was he an avatar to Cernunnos, or was Cernunnos a son to Cernonson, who is really Cernon himself?

Time has passed, so many eons that we'll never know for sure. At least that is how I perceive it to be. Would Gwyn and her people recognize the concept yet? How long after we left them did their descendants trap themselves into that postulate?

What we know is that long-ago peoples, perhaps a people from before those we recognize as "human" came to be, had a revered figure who resembled a stag man in appearance. Sometimes they depicted him as having antlers on a human head and body. Other times, they depicted him as having a full stag's head on a human body.

He always had the antlers. Huge antlers. So huge that many descendants, when they lost remembrance of what he represented, sought to slay the great deer that they encountered for the glory of their antlers. "This one has the most tines," they would say. "Yet, this one masses far larger," others would claim.

None who sought the antlers remembered to honor the bucks and bulls that gave their lives so that man could eat; could cover their bare bodies for warmth; could survive. None remembered that there was once a god who travelled with the most ancient of men, guiding their paths, warning them of impending dangers.

How did those memories die? Am I brave enough to travel with Cernon again to learn that answer?

When Matthew's forces besieged Jamari and me up on Milltown Hill, at the very heart of the Founder's Glade, it was Cernon who came to our aid. He and his people.

He could have been many things to those ancient peoples, but this tale is what Cernon is to me. To the Elk Creek Tribe of the year 2174 CE. To the future of mankind.

Through my reading, I relate Cernunnos to the Tuatha Dé Danann, the Children of Danaan in English. Danaan (Danu by name) was a goddess of the Celts in pre-Milesian mythology. This was many centuries after the birth of my Cernonson and happened on an isle where my tribe would have crossed as they navigated the ice age to the Americas.

I suspect Cernonson is the father of the legendary Cernunnos. And Cernon is the grandfather of them all.

Using legends, old tales, and even rumors of tales, I built what seems a logical sequence to how my ancient tribe came to America.

Danu was the leader of a people who of many Fae forms. The stag-man is but one. It is this familial membership which separates Cernunnos from Cernon. Cernunnos fled to the British Isles with the other Tuatha Dé Danaan when the Romans overtook the Continent and destroyed the pagan "superstitions" of the Stone-age world.

Long before Cernunnos made that exodus, though, Cernonson had become just Cernon again and had guided His people across the ice floes of the ancient Atlantic Ocean of 50-plus thousand years ago. This was long before there was a Bronze Age, and His people then were tribal and nomadic.

Of the Tuath Dé Danann, in those ancient times, well into the Bronze Age, the Celts and their gods were a dominant force across all lands on the European continent.

Cernon, though, had another tale. Cernon stayed in the icy lands of the north when Cernunnos traveled south and then, eventually, west to the British Islands.

For untold thousands of years, Cernon led his people through the harsh wildernesses and fjords. Then one eon, there was ice across the entire ocean. This wasn't ice as told of in the crossing the Siberian land bridge, but flows of ice which Cernon's humans ventured out onto using a combination of seal-skin boats and woven snow shoes. Eventually, they found a new land on a far-off continent. Iceland.

Some say the mythical Isle of Avalon is the land where Cernon went, and for thousands of years, that was the tale. Then we met our Cernon and our understanding expanded.

Cernon had seers and shamans who listened to him as each age of mankind advanced. His people marched further west on that icy continent until one day he was at the far edges of the world looking across another ocean where maybe on a still and cloudless day they could see the darker blue on the horizon that told of another land, yet. Greenland. So on they went in their descending generations.

The tribe he led found no comfort in the lands of Greenland, so they ventured across yet another expanse. No one can say how long ago they arrived, but they arrived in America, stepping off of the ice floes and onto a larger continent than they had ever suspected.

The Tuatha Dé Cernon travelled south into warmer climes. The humans and the Fae both thrived for thousands of years in the American north and west, fathering a continent of people who claimed that land for tens of thousands of years.

When another race overran the mass of descendants of our little tribe, they forbid the remnants to remember the lore of their ancestors.

Cernon became a forgotten god. He dwindled from the greatness he had once enjoyed and eventually lost the ability to take physical form. He endured a spectral existence for two centuries before Founder Knight found him and the two became friends as they watched the tiny community build itself up in Milltown, just up Elk Creek, from the tiny hamlet of North Douglas.

Then they reached out to Jamari when they saw he could perceive them. That is when Jamari and I restored the Tuatha Dé Cernon back into the world.

***

Chapter Thirteen

The Long Walk Home

Gwyniffred felt her age as she awakened from a long night. The rest of her people were up and about, and the hunters had already left on their daily quest for food. She regretted that her family was taking for granted that she needed more sleep than they did. She regretted it was true and what it meant for her future. At thirty-three, she was the oldest member of the tribe. She recognized that her end days were near.

She took a pine-bark cup of willow tea offered by her middle granddaughter and sipped the foul-tasting brew, thanking the long-vanished Sophia for sharing the secret of its pain-relieving properties.

As she sipped the concoction, she walked out of the cave entrance and looked out. The spring thaw was long over-due, and she hoped to see the ice melting at last. She was disappointed yet again, though. It looked like even more snow had come in the night. And if she looked closely, she could see that the glacier above had encroached even closer to the cave mouth. For years, they had watched the glacier in its relentless march, wondering when it would stop.

Looking at the new snow and seeing the blue ice even more adamant in its advance than ever before, she realized that the cave itself, as a home and a refuge, was in its last days as well. When she looked down the slope toward the creek, she saw the gatherers returning. Her son Cernunnos was leading them and she could see the shadowy presence of Cernonson at his side. Both of them looked up at the same time and paused as they saw her sipping her tea. She saw them look at each other, seeing regret and simultaneous acceptance between the two.

They had made some decision, she realized. And it had to be a decision to move on from their long-held home. She decided she could not make the journey with them even as she realized that was the regret she had seen in their shared look.

Gwyniffred had never felt the same sense of sharing as she had enjoyed during the few months when Sophia had shared her body, but when her two sons were together, and of one mind, it was very close to the same thing. The three of them had just realized together that she would remain in this cave for her last days while the tribe sought a better future.

They would leave for better lands. She would not.

They settled it long before the two finished their short walk up to the cave entrance. It was a done deal before the tribe had gathered to hear their plan.

She made sure none saw her dash tears from her eyes as she moved to pick up a breakfast bone to gnaw on as the tribal chief, her son, resplendent in long red hair and snapping blue eyes, looked around his gathered people.

"We must move," he told them in the guttural voice and arm gestures of their language.

"The ice advances. Even the longer days of the year could not stop its march." He gestured up to the towering blue wall above their cave. "Cernonson tells me that the ice will enclose the cave mouth in the coming year. We can never hold it back. Already we have to limit our fires within because of the loss of chimney openings above. We are freezing in our furs at night and we must recognize the danger before the ice takes us."

Cernunnos looked at Cernonson, knowing that only Wainson and his mother, the great vision-seeker, could also see their spirit guide. "We must take what we can pack within the next hand of days and carry it with us on a journey to a far-off place. The trip will be difficult and we will lose many on the way. But Cernonson tells me his father, the great Cernon, has told him there is a warm and dry land awaiting. A land we will spread across and grow; where we will become many tribes of many nations over tens of thousands of seasons."

A hand span of days later, Gwyniffred watched the last of her family round the last bend far below the cave mouth. Then she looked up at the blue ice looming over her. "Take me if you can," she muttered to the inanimate force. "I'll go when it's my time and not a moment sooner."

She walked inside, seeing the lone hearth smoking in the darkness. Shuffling slowly over, she added some dry sticks to bring the flames dancing up. Then her eyes beheld the ochre painting of Cernon and Sophia on the wall. Remembering that long-ago day when Cernon and Sophia first entered their cave, she resolved to spend her last days grinding the earlier image into the rock face. Whatever happened, whenever the ice relented, whether it be a hundred years hence or an unimaginable ten thousand, there would be a record of the tribe of Cernunnos.

She looked at the piled heap of bags stacked in the back of the cavern over the years. They had collected more meat than what the tribe could carry on their final exodus. There was pemmican enough for her to live another dozen years. And beside that stack was wood enough to feed her fire for even longer.

She settled a fur around her shoulders and set herself up in front of the wall, lifting a pointed stone up and scratching Sophia's face. Over and over again, she followed the ochre lines, letting tendrils of sand fall on her lap as she worked until she permanently embedded her spirit-sister's face in bas-relief. She looked up to find the day over and darkness long since fallen. The fire had died down to dull embers and her old bones were quaking in the chill.

She heard as well as felt her knees creak as she stood, and she had to hold still against a sudden dizziness. She wondered how much of that image she could embed into the wall before she could no longer get up. Then she stepped over and added wood to the fire. From the leather bags nearby, she set up a tripod to heat water, dropping a hot stone into it right away.

Waiting for the water to warm enough to soften the pemmican, she went to the cave mouth by habit, looking out as if to find her tribe coming home from a long hunt, even knowing they would never round the bend of the stream below again. The stars were out in a vast scattering of jewels, reminding her just how small she really was. From the distance, she heard a wolf howl and then a yipping crescendo as a pack formed for the night's hunt.

She pushed the logs into place to block the opening, draping hides over them and bracing other branches in place to prevent any wolf or tiger from making its way into her home in the night. She felt the small breeze as air forced its way in to feed the fire and carry the smoke up the lone remaining chimney. The fire bloomed in the freshet and she settled in to make her lonely dinner.

The next day, she left the cave and gathered pigments. Then, she returned to her work on the frieze.

This became the pattern of her days. She didn't even stop to think that it had been weeks since she had looked out the cave mouth. There would be no one returning to check on her. Gwyniffred was alone with the images which were growing into the wall. She picked up a piece of white chalk and used it to lighten Sophia's fur robe. She used a darker stone to color Cernon's russet mane.

When the fire danced across their visages, the dancing shadow and light awakened them enough to give her a show of life. The flickering flames reminded her of the day Sophia had held little Cernonson to her breast, so she added a little blue-eyed, flame-haired babe suckling at the spirit-woman's bosom.

Then one day the air no longer pushed in through the hanging hides at the door. The smoke no longer travelled up the chimney but lingered in a foul cloud in the cave. Keeping the fire small kept the smoke from coming all the way to the floor and she could breathe the air, even though it wasn't offering her as much renewal as she hoped for.

She crawled to the door and lifted the hide. Behind the log barrier was a blue wall of ice. She could see hazy shadows shifting behind the glare, but there was no air coming in and there was no way to open a path through the glacier.

Gwyniffred stood despite a bout of dizziness, letting it pass. "So, you've got me," she said. "As you always were going to do."

She turned back to the fire. It smoldered as if it, too, couldn't draw enough life from the stale air. To the slumbering stack, she added sticks to generate enough glow that the image of Cernon and Sophia come to life a last time in the dancing shadows.

***

Sophia had long settled back into her routine in Milltown Hall. She had almost forgotten about her journey to the far distant tribe who were facing the onslaught of the ice age. They had long ago deposed Matthew as Chief Elk Creek and Elan was now chief. Jamari had been gone from this realm for years. Sophia wondered why she didn't move up the hill to her children.

Then one evening, as she walked back toward her rooms after lunch, there was a commotion from the front entry. A whispering susurrus spread from the doors and lifted into a near-roar of excited voices.

Then she heard the clacking of hooves on stone. Sophia knew that sound. It was the sound Cernon's hooves had made when he once moved across the ancient cave floor during that long ago journey.

The sudden silence from the people was deafening, highlighting the clop-clop-clop of the visitor's advance. She could sense fear and awe from those in the hallway as they paused in their walk from dinner and out to the various branches of the great Hall for their evening activities. The clopping echoed up the hall and then became even louder as the traveler turned up the hall toward her abode.

She knew from the whitened faces turned toward her and then back around the bend who it was. She couldn't imagine why Cernon would have broken his long isolation; couldn't even think what it meant that he showed himself in the hall of the Elk Creek Tribe, and why he headed toward her quarters. But it was the only answer to the sounds and the awed shock on the surrounding faces.

Then Cernon rounded the bend. He held his head low to keep his antlers from scraping the tall ceiling of the carved hallway. His feet dragged and slid as a result, and the clopping had become less pronounced. Even more alarming was the determination on his face as he saw her. The whites of his eyes showed his discomfort with being on dead stone, away from the spirit-connection to his forests.

He held out his hand, beckoning her to him. She stepped obediently forward to the awe of her fellow tribesmen. They had long known that the gods had chosen her. But to have one of those great ones come to the hall to summon her was beyond any expectation. Many bowed down toward the pair, and she felt certain that she was just as much honored as he.

"We have a journey to make," Cernon told her. "It is time for us to bring home one of our own."

Jamari, was her sudden thought. Was he coming home from walking with the gods after these many decades?

"You will remember her as Gwyniffred," Cernon said as he took her hand and led her off into the deeper tunnels of Milltown Hall. She wondered at his destination as he led her down several flights of stairs that she had never known of. Then he opened a massive stone door, and she felt a buffeting of cool, damp air and smelled the mustiness of a mushroom farm.

Mycelium, she realized. Cernon and his people's connection to the world. There was a crypt in the very bowels of Milltown Hall that she had never known of. He was taking her back to that long ago time and suddenly she recoiled. Must she travel that path again? Must she witness Gwyniffred's end?

Once his hooves reached the mushroom base, Cernon stopped and sighed out his relief at being re-connected to his essence. She could sense him stretch out his senses, could feel his awareness reach out to the wider world via the mycelium network. "Focus on me," he instructed her, the same as he had done all those years gone. "Don't let your focus waver for a moment. We both must be there to bring her home."

Then he drew her in, crashing into the maelstrom of prisming kaleidoscoping light. Again, the onslaught of visual rage overwhelmed her. Like falling into a black hole must be, she thought. She cried out her panic when she realized she had lost focus on Cernon, but quickly grasped back onto his presence when she sought him. He had held her intact through the lapse.

She fell in a heap onto a dark floor when they emerged from the journey. When she had recovered enough, she saw firelight flickering on a cave wall. The old image from that first day seemed far more substantial now.

The Sophia image there still had the faint suggestion of horns but now sported a pale robe of furs and it held a red-headed babe. She gasped aloud at the image, wondering how it could be.

There was a slow shuffle from a still form on the floor. When she looked down, she saw Gwyniffred reaching up an aged and feeble hand to them. "I see my spirit sister. You've come to see me off," Gwyniffred said. "I won't have to go alone."

"No, you won't be going alone," Cernon reassured her. "You will come along with us to a far distant land. You'll get to see the home that has drawn your people, and there make your rest with your descendants."

Sophia reached her hand down to meet that of Gwyniffred's. It was so cold in hers, so still and fragile.

"Stand," Cernon ordered her. "Let us behold your final work together."

When Gwyniffred obeyed that command, her spirit form stood, leaving the shell of her body behind in the furs.

The three looked at the images of Cernon and Sophia with her baby. Gwyniffred had carved them into the cave wall deeply enough to last centuries beyond count.

The last flickers of flame died out as they consumed the last oxygen in the cavern. Then darkness enveloped them beyond all imagining.

"We must go now," Cernon said. Sophia experienced the pull into the maelstrom of time and space again. This time she was the one holding Gwyniffred into the group, keeping her from shredding away in the storm.

When they arrived at their destination, she found herself at a familiar place up in the forest above Milltown Hall. They were standing next to the tree she herself had traveled down to the Redwood Forest to gather. When she brought it here, she intended it to be her ultimate resting place. This was where she would have her body laid down when she passed.

That had been over twenty years before. Now the redwood seedling of that long ago time had sprouted up to fifty feet tall and was about ten inches in diameter. She had brought a batch of redwood seedlings home for the retreat she and Jamari set up in the Founder's Grove. Those trees were prospering still and were doing even better than this lone one, which she had set into place a half mile down the hill toward Milltown Hall. She chose this species because they lived and would keep growing for thousands of years.

When the trio recovered from the journey, Sophia and Cernon, now in their physical bodies, looked to the spirit form of Gwyniffred. "I planted this tree to hold my final spirit," Sophia told her. "I seem to be lasting much longer than I thought I would. If you would like, you are welcome to reside here and I will join you when I pass into the ancestor's realm and we can be soul sisters again, as we were so long ago."

The spirit form of Gwyn looked at Sophia, tears in her eyes. "Yes, I would like that." She looked around the wood, seeing new trees and not a shred of snow or ice. "What place is this? Are my people here?"

"This is the continent your people came to after hundreds of seasons of travail," Cernon told her. "The trees of this forest are home to many of their spirit essences. Others have gone beyond Gaia on missions for the Great Spirit."

Gwyniffred reached a spectral hand toward the young tree. "Will you come and visit me?" she asked Sophia.

"Oh, yes." Sophia said. "I want to learn all the things that became of our tribe after I saw you last. We have so much to catch up with!"

Gwyniffred moved to and into Sophia. It wasn't a complete connection as they had once shared, but it was enough that Sophia heard her thoughts faintly. A home in the warmth, her spirit sister said as she stepped into the tree.

Sophia and Cernon watched her spirit essence grow to fill a new body. They both sensed a sigh of wonder and contentment as the tree seemed to swell with renewed energy.

Sophia let tears run down her face as she reached out to caress the rough bark. She felt a questing sigh from within, then turned away.

"How much longer must I dwell here in the dream world before joining her, I wonder?" the nearly 100-year-old woman in a fifty-year-old looking body asked.

"You're still trying to force yourself into some constant time line," Cernon admonished her. "Your spirit will know when it is time to rest." He reached an arm around her for a gentle hug, and she looked up to see tears welling in his eyes as well. "Until then, there seems to be a new story to build into your memoirs."

Epilogue

***

A cave in northern Norway

The Euro News

A new find in northern Norway could shatter the history of the world as we learned it. A group of hikers were bold enough to venture into a cave revealed in a small temblor recently. The hikers were the first to venture into the treacherous gorge since the most recent quakes had sloughed off the cliff-faces.

They had defied guidelines to wait even longer for fear of more avalanches. They felt sure that the quakes had settled, as the last aftershock had been a barely perceptible 2.6 and over a week before.

When they saw the dark opening of a new cave, they were nervous to approach, but then they saw what looked like images on one of the visible walls. A settlement of ancient man!

When they saw the subject of the frieze, they were confused. Here was a Cernunnos figure, with horns sporting from a human head, wearing furs, which was unusual in the extreme, but even more impossible was his human companion. She wore white furs in the imagery and held a red-haired, blue-eyed baby at her breast.

According to the explorers' reports, it looked as if the ancient artist had placed a diminutive set of antlers on her head but then had erased them, leaving only a ghostly image.

Some photos which were secreted out seem to show a mummified body laying below the frieze. We have met silence on all requests for images and reports. No one is answering questions down at the precinct, and they have ordered the university investigators to silence.

Authorities report there will be an investigation of this cave. Too many questions evolve from the images and the mummified remains. They suspect someone has raided the site at some earlier time or that some group of errant teens put up wall-art in jest. Was there some long-past infiltrator who left mis-leading clues?

The obvious age of the remains in the cave, along with the condition and clarity of the depictions, seems most authentic. More importantly, the frieze matched works found in caves further to the south from around 50,000 years before.

The local constabulary placed the site off limits and placed rope barriers and signs warning of a new find. And they've left armed guards at the canyon entrance.

We will keep you updated on the new discovery. Is it a real find, or is someone having a colossal joke on mankind?

The End

Final Notes:

Every thesaurus and dictionary I can find tells me there is no such word as prisming. Yet, I will use it in this work because it conveys the best "sense" of what I want to convey. Yes, I could use "refracting" but it doesn't give the "feel" of what I want it to give where prisming does.

So there. Author's right.

The World of Paradigm Lost

The author recommends reading the books of Paradigm Lost in the order below:

Cernon

Heretic

In a culture where the government constantly feeds the sludge of doctrine and thinking into your ear buds, one young man is asked to go into the wilderness. A wilderness where technology is anathema and his ear buds burn until he removes them. Then he has to learn to think for himself.

Justice Preston begins a new assignment as a priest of the Church of Jamari in the year 3117 CE. He travels far from his home to Milltown Village, the ancient home of The Jamari with the assignment to dig out any information he can about Jamari's miracles. His mentor, now the Supreme Bishop of the Church of Jamari, has tasked him to look into the rumored presence of the Fae living with the Children of Jamari in the wilderness around the Founder's Grove also.

He is licensed to study the ancient rite of shamanism, but there hasn't been a known or licensed shaman in the village for decades to teach him.

Can he take on these practices on his own? Is there a wild shaman, as the Supreme Bishop Omnia seems to have suggested, who will step forward to guide him?

Jamari and the Manhood Rites

In the year 2115, Jamari is a young man readying himself to enter the Manhood Rites so he can become a full adult in the Elk Creek Tribe. As young Jamari learns of his culture via these rites, the reader is along for the lessons as well. The world around Milltown is still recovering from the great quakes of 2040 CE and many areas are still unpopulated after the tsunamis and quakes devastated them.

Manhood Rites Trilogy Page
https://www.amazon.com/Jamari-Manhood-Rites-3-Book/dp/B07HYMVKMY

Jamari Shaman

Young Jamari, while participating in the Manhood Rites, encounters a hawk floating above the wintry land. He imagines himself to be seeing from the hawk's eyes and suddenly finds himself on a shamanic vision journey.

He is recognized as a shaman and asked to begin training into an entire new life direction. He must leave his dreams of being a tribal leader behind and accept a new type of greatness. One that demands far more of his very soul. One that can bring even higher conquests, but also death to those who can't make it.

This novel was built as a stand-alone and the author chose several chapters from the first work in the series to become Chapters One through Three. If you've already read that first novel, you can begin this one on Chapter Four.

The Founder's Sons

Jamari is near completion of the four years of Manhood Rites. He is regarded as one of the most admired of tribal shamans, called "God Walker" after his recent exploits. He leaves the sadness of a profound loss behind as he steps into adulthood.

There is a vision haunting him. A very clear dream of talking to a stag-man who guides him up to the Founder's Grave where he is asked to perform a ritual.

He's been recently appointed as the tribe's Knight Shaman, the highest leader of shamans in the tribe, yet still takes Terry, the most recent Knight Shaman on his biggest ventures. Also with him on this journey is the Sophia Shaman, the female version of the Knight Shaman, and ranked equal to him. As well, there is Elan and Haloki, a dedicated couple who seek to use the ceremony to consecrate their relationship.

Jamari and the Sophia Shaman enact a ceremony to awaken Founder Knight's essence into the tree he had designated for that role when he passed 80 years ago. It is during this ceremony that the greatest miracle of all occurs.

Eros Times, Part I

Tales of Jamari's days that were deemed far too explicit for inclusion in the novels.

https://www.amazon.com/Paradigm-Lost-Times-Stories-Creek-ebook/dp/B01N5XQKRU

Night Studies, Eros Times II

A more structured and detailed story of Jamari's adventures in the Night Studies. Some have described the scenes within as a series of how-to lessons in the art of sexual loving.

https://www.amazon.com/Night-Studies-Times-Stories-Creek-ebook/dp/B09X5SKXS4

The Sophia Shaman

This is the gathered writings (not all of them!) that led Justice Preston down the road to heresy and exile. It has many fun and revealing stories, but is not a true novel in that there's no real plot. The Sophia Shaman wrote these in her later years, long after she had relinquished the tribal role of the Sophia Shaman to another. They were hidden away within the first few years of having been written as they told raw truths about the Jamari, truths that often decried the new religion being built up in his name.

When Justice found the original hand-written copies hidden away in the ancient keep, his path was sealed. The world would never be the same.

From Heretic

After finishing their meal, they left Milltown Hall and walked down to the footbridge to cross the river. Justice paused as they passed by the Jamari Tree. It had only been a few weeks since he even learned that

Jamari's totem pole miracle tree was still alive, yet he couldn't imagine a world where it wasn't. Keeping his reverence short, he sent well-wishes to the tree and its surrounding offspring. Then they turned up the trail beside the dam and hiked to the edge of the Ancestor's Grove.

"How far do you think we should go?" Justice asked.

"I know a small clearing near the top," Ian answered. He reached for and held Justice's hand to lead the way. "It should be perfect. Did you remember the rattle?"

Justice patted the carisack at his side and they both heard the muffled sound from within. Justice enjoyed the warmth of Ian's hand in his own. It was the perfect touch as he finally walked through the ancient glade; in harmony with his lover as he experienced the awe of this ancient and revered place. He saw some of the oldest Oak trees he had ever seen in his life. They were all different, each gnarled with age, sending twisted limbs reaching above the forest floor. They had to duck under an occasional outthrust limb and often had to break their hand hold, but each time Justice exulted when Ian reached back for him again.

About ten minutes into the walk, he saw a brightening in the wood ahead. The hill was gradual, yet the pace still left him winded. When Ian headed straight for the apparent opening, he slowed to catch his breath. Then they entered a clearing left when a tree had died. It looked as if it had died hundreds of years ago, leaving a snaggled carcass sporting many truncated limbs splayed in all directions. None of the other trees had expanded their growth to fill the void.

When he ran his hand over the remnants, he felt life, as if its neighbors were feeding it their own sap. If he believed trees were capable of human-type emotion and connection, he would think they were showing respect for this perished giant. Maybe he believed it. From his reading of Jamari's life, Jamari certainly did.

Justice pulled a blanket out of his bag, dislodging the gourd rattle in a dissonant clatter. He laid the blanket out over the flattest part of the depression left by the uplifted root wad and then pulled out a ceramic bowl, some sage, and a lighter. "I wanted to do this the last time," he said, "but I didn't want to smoke up my rooms."

"I wonder if we should," Ian answered quietly as he glanced furtively around the small meadow grown around the downed ancient.

Justice, thinking Ian was still hesitant about the shamanistic practices, saw him looking around the greensward as if he were uncomfortable. "You look nervous," Justice said. "I know how big a thing it is that you're helping me, and I want you to know how much I appreciate it. Do you want to back out? I don't want to push you into something you're not ready for."

"No. It's okay," Ian answered quickly. "I was just worried about the flame. It is late summer and dry, even though we are near a rain forest."

"I thought about that," Justice said, pulling out a stoppered bottle of water. "The blanket is fire resistant. The bowl should contain any sparks, and we can quickly douse anything that gets out with the water if necessary."

Ian looked around the small opening in the wood, still seeming anxious. "Okay," he said, "I just didn't expect you to use this process is all."

"I learned about this cleansing process in Sophia's journals," Justice said, "while reading 'The Founder's Sons.' That is one tome in the Sophia's collection, though I think she didn't originally write it. I mean, the one I have, she wrote. Just as she wrote all the others, but there are details she wouldn't have known about. Anyway, it is the third one about Jamari's early life. It has a lot of details that were left out of the Jamari Bible. I don't want to eliminate any of the process that they used since I don't know enough to wing it on my own yet."

Justice realized he was dithering and shrugged off his own discomfort, nodding to Ian as an apology. At the back of his mind, the events of the morning were still digging at him. The realization that he was defying the church was gnawing even further into his concentration. He hoped the ritualized process would divert his rational self from obsessing over minute details.

As he laid out the items, Justice turned to the north and stood. He closed his eyes to banish extraneous thought. All those concerns would still be there later if his overself needed to keep digging at them.

"I'm counting on you for so much," he said, opening his eyes and looking into Ian's. "That doesn't mean that you're obligated to follow through with my actions, though. Sophia and Jamari both could journey without rattle or drum, and I can attempt to do the same if needed." He gave Ian a chance to say something, to back out, or to find an excuse to move on.

"I'm with you for this venture," Ian said. "Will you allow me to complete the ritual while you clear your mind and focus?"

Justice squatted to place the water and bowl between them. "Yes," he said. "I would be glad for your help. You have more experience in these matters than I, so I'll take your advice and follow it." He lifted the bundle of sage and the lighter to Ian.

Ian leaned over and held the bundle of sage over the dish and lighted it. He let the open flame consume part of the mass before blowing forcefully onto it, directing his breath, and any resultant sparks, down onto the blanket. When this quenched the flames, he made sure that the sage was still smoldering, puffing lightly on the mass to encourage the heat. When the smoke intensified and the twisted edges showed red tendrils curling around the fodder, the sage bundle was ready. "You should close your eyes and clear your conscious mind," Ian directed.

Justice closed his eyes and breathed in the scent of the smoky herb, trying not to breathe the aromatic herb too deeply and start a coughing fit as Ian wove the smoke around his face.

"Open your eyes and follow me through this next part," Ian said. Justice opened his eyes to witness Ian reaching the smoldering bundle to the east. "Watchtower of the east, land of the rising sun and new beginnings, guard this rite." Then he turned to the south. "Land of the mid-day sun, passion and fire, shed your light on this man's journey that he may find his path." Ian smoothly continued his turning, now facing west. "Land of the setting sun, home of the dying day, let your power of contemplation reach Justice in his journey." Then he turned back to the north. "Land of connection, home of the soul, lend your strength that Justice may find his path within."

Having made the space sacred, Ian finished out the rite, focusing on the day's goal. "All who can hear, witness and aid Justice's journey to his spirit guide. Look over and protect him as he quests his spirit out to the deep places. Bring him home safe when his mission is complete. Ancestors of this glade, I ask your blessing for this journey."

Justice settled down onto the blanket and looked to Ian. He gestured to the gourd and nodded for Ian to begin the rhythm.

Ian ground the sage into the dish, being sure to snuff out all heat and spark, then sat down as well and picked up the rattle. He began with a slow cadence.

Justice let his eyes fall closed, hands relaxing on his knees as he let the rhythmic energy lull him into vision. "I seek my Spirit Guide," he muttered half aloud. "I hope for guidance on a dangerous path." Then, instead of envisioning climbing down the roots of the Jamari Tree, he thought of the roots of the ancient tree he was now under; thought of finding an opening between trunk and ground, perhaps of a chipmunk, and crawling into that burrow to start his downward journey.

Entering the journey, he perceived the roots, which he had thought would be dead and rotting, seemed instead to be vibrantly glowing as if lighting a green-gold path down to the Lower World. This time, he expected the headlong rush as he accelerated his downward slide. The glow of the root structure faded to blackness, and he lost the smell and feel of earthen contact. Then he saw a dim glow approaching as he slid deeper into the transition.

Unlike the previous journey, Justice alighted in a lively copse this time. The feel was of an open meadow, with a small clump of trees in the center where he arrived. Flowers of varying color and hue sprung up through meadow grasses, exuding scent and pollen onto a gentle wind.

"I seek my Spirit Guide. Is my Spirit Guide here to meet me?"

There was a sudden swelling from a nearby clump of ferns and the stagman of his earlier vision stood from a newly formed opening into this Lower World. "I greet you, Justice of the Church of Jamari," his guide spoke as he stepped nearer.

Justice saw that his earlier impression of the diminutive size of his guide must have been off. He now appeared to have the same height as Justice himself, with his spread out antlers lifting his essence even higher. "I greet you, my Spirit Guide," Justice replied. "Do you have a name you could share with me?"

The stagman paused. In surprise or alarm, Justice couldn't discern. "We don't give our true name lightly," he answered sternly. "You can call me Blackdeer, though, and that will be enough."

"You honor me, Blackdeer," Justice answered. "Having a name to call you by is a blessing."

"It is the way of kinship," Blackdeer replied. "I have long awaited your arrival."

"How long could you have been waiting?" Justice queried. "I only recently realized spirit journeying was a possibility."

"The separation between the worlds has grown tenuous since the Jamari Days," Blackdeer answered. "And time in our realm differs from yours." He paused, looking around the small glade they were in. "There is more to your story than you know." He paused again, seeming to decide whether to share that extra tale. "I am normally found in the Middle World, yet when I felt you travelling to the Lower last week, I moved to meet you. And again today, I moved to meet you."

Blackdeer perused the small glade again. "We've created a delightful place together," he said in approval. "I think we'll always meet here, though we'll build it in the Middle World where I am most comfortable. Just come to the same place in your world when you want to find me, then 'journey' to the Middle World instead of the Lower."

Justice then looked around as Blackdeer had done and recognized that he was standing in the shade of the same tree he had started his journey from. Only in this world, it still lived.

Blackdeer looked back at Justice. "You mentioned 'enlightenment for coming days' as you invoked the goodwill of the ancestors. What guidance are you seeking for a future yet unknown?"

The question set justice back, not even remembering what he had asked for at first. Then, as he remembered what he had said, he clarified for Blackdeer. "I've found some undiscovered writings from The Sophia," he said. "In those, I've learned that the Church of Jamari has hidden much from her followers. They have obscured even the fact of journeying to meet a spirit guide. I've started writing out many of the things Sophia shared."

He looked into Blackdeer's dark eyes, glad that here was yet another he could share his burdens with. "You referred to me as 'of the Church of Jamari.' When the church discovers my heresy, I fear they'll try to eliminate me." He stopped to consider again. "Not that I fear my death, having discovered these Other Worlds. I am now sure that I will go on, that the church can't stop my spirit, even after my mortal body passes. But there are so very many who do not have that reassurance, who still fear that the condemnation of the church is also the extinguishment of the soul. I would bring The Sophia's words to them so that they too may be free."

"It's a very large goal," Blackdeer said, considering. Then he looked intently into Justice's eyes. "A way forward is going to come to you much sooner than you realize."

"What does that mean?" Justice queried.

"Only that there will be someone coming to you soon who will lead you to another path," Blackdeer answered with a reassuring, maybe even mischievous, smile. "I have the pleasure of being your guide when you seek answers from the spirit realms. This other will guide you in your Dream World."

Justice recalled Sophia referring to the physical world as the Dream World as well. He thought of the words of Wolf when He spoke to Jen, informing her that her world must be a Dream World since Wolf himself lived in the Lower World and only rarely ventured to that other space.

Blackdeer looked up as the realm darkened. "I think your partner is calling you back," he said as Justice, too, sensed a change around him.

"I'm not ready to return yet!" Justice exclaimed.

"We'll meet again, I assure you," Blackdeer said as the new beat of the rattle pulled Justice away from that space. "Don't be surprised when you return to them!"

Who could he mean by "them?" Justice wondered as he opened his eyes to see Ian frantically shaking the gourd in a rapid and broken rhythm and staring at his face. As Ian recognized his conscious return, he stopped his frantic shaking of the gourd. "You're back," he said. Then he stopped and looked behind Justice, above the level of his head. He gazed back down at Justice. "I want you to meet someone," he said as he motioned behind.

Justice heard a soft rustling as of grasses bending under a new foot and twisted around to see who it was. He saw a youngish-looking man, naked, and with ram's horns growing from his brow. Startled, he tumbled into a forward roll and away. When he reached Ian, he turned to face the creature while still crouching. Then he felt back with his hand to be sure Ian was behind him and safe.

"Don't be alarmed!" Ian said, catching him and holding him in both arms. "This is Berkhold. He has been wanting to meet you for some time now."

Justice stared at the apparition before him. Boyish face, complete with an abundance of freckles and an upturned pug nose. Curly chestnut hair parted around small ram's horns to either side. A hairless chest above a trim belly with only a smattering of hairs leading down to… well, that certainly wasn't boyish. He was human down to his naked groin, but with goat's legs and cloven hooves.

"Pleased to meet you," Berkhold greeted him.

"I thought I had come back from my vision journey," Justice stammered. "How is it you're here in my vision, Ian? How is it that this new spirit guide greets me?"

"Shh. It's okay," Ian reassured him, still holding him in both arms. "You are back. This is the real world. Only it has more to it than they've allowed you to know before. Berkhold is only one of many new denizens you'll get to meet soon."

Justice could feel his racing heart subside. He had broken out in a sudden sweat, which now cooled his entire body to goose bumps, and his fluttering stomach was settling as well. He stopped pushing back with his legs and took a long look at Berkhold.

The faun wasn't nearly as intimidating as he seemed at first. He was probably a couple of inches shorter than Ian and had a very slight build. The boyish face also carried through his body. Other than the upstanding manhood, he was more like a stripling lad than an intimidating apparition.

"Sorry for the fright," Berkhold offered. "Can I help you up so we can visit?"

"Um. Sure," Justice answered, reaching out to take the faun's offered hand. Berkhold's strength was surprising for the slight build as Justice felt himself lifted quickly. Berkhold's hand was warm against Justice's. Perhaps because Justice was still damp and clammy from his fright. Then he was looking down into Berkhold's upturned face.

"You're a damn sight taller than I expected," Berkhold offered in his boyish voice. "I hope that reassures you some."

Justice felt his voice break with nervousness as he returned the greeting. "I'm sorry," he said. "I don't know how it's even possible that you're here in physical form in my Dream World, as I've heard it called."

"You'll get all the explanation you could hope for once you meet the Arawn," Berkhold answered him. "He was sharing your dream with Blackdeer as you conversed and will greet you now as well."

"Who is 'the Arawn?'" Justice asked, letting himself relax again after the fright.

"It's not who, so much as 'what,'" Berkhold answered. "The Arawn is the king of the Tuath Dé. That is what we call ourselves, those of us who have come through the veil to your world. I don't mind it too much, but the others are resentful of being called 'the Faerie' and it would be best if you didn't do so."

"You're the fabled Fair Folk?" Justice asked in amazement.

"Not the Fair Folk," Berkhold replied, "the Tuath Dé. You may get to meet the Fair Folk soon as well."

Berkhold paused and looked to Ian. "You are going to be granted an audience with the Children of Jamari," he told him. "In the next week or two, one of us will meet you and escort you up to the Founder's Grove, where they live."

"Really? After all this time?" Ian answered. "I had about given up and was going to ask Justice to seek exile with me down in Elkton."

"That would be a terrible idea," said a deep and thundering voice from behind Justice.

He whipped around, fighting the inclination to put himself between the owner of that voice and Ian. Then all thought of any such action swept out of his mind as he saw a ten-foot tall stagman who was obviously of elk origin instead of Blacktail Deer, as his own spirit guide was. Ian, still seated, reached for Justice's hand for an assist and turned as he stood.

"Greetings, Cernon, hail and well met," Ian said respectfully. "May I present my friend, Justice, under-priest of the Church of Jamari?"

Cernon! This must be the one The Sophia had written of when she described her journey to a far distant past!

Justice quailed at the intensity of the look this creature gave him. He didn't dare to ask this being if he were the one Sophia had written of. His stern face was intimidation incarnate. Though his beard was sparse, in the manner of some human races, his mien was resolute.

Justice stuttered but could think of nothing appropriate to say. This was human immensity over a tawny coat of elk fur with the darkened guard hairs below the naked groin. Where Berkhold was unadorned and naked, Cernon wore shoulder shields which were held in place with crossed leather belts that ran down to a waist belt. He had adorned these pauldrons with silver filigreed studs and they were wider than the already-broad shoulders. The crossed leather bands held scabbards with knives that appeared to be made of bone, along with a stone axe. The belt below held a long sword that seemed to be as long as Justice was tall.

"Welcome to our home," Cernon greeted Justice. "We would have invited you sooner, but there were some other details we needed to tend to first."

Cernon then looked at Ian, even more stern than before. "Our names are gifts we choose to grant and only ours to give," he reprimanded. "If we thought you knew our customs better, you'd face punishment for that breach."

"I am sorry," Ian said, bowing his head. "Your sudden appearance surprised me. Even though Berkhold seems to materialize out of thin air so many times, I can't get used to how the Tuath Dé can do this thing."

"It's of no importance for this time," Cernon answered. "I had planned to gift Justice with my name, anyway." He turned back to Justice.

"I travelled the spirit world with Founder Knight through his many years there before coming into this world to share his new journey when he returned."

"Founder Knight still lives? After a thousand years?" Justice asked, his eyes widening in shock.

"Yes. But not as you may expect," Cernon answered. "You'll learn more detail later. There is a great deal you've yet to learn before being granted that high honor."

Cernon looked to Berkhold then. "This is enough for a first meeting," he instructed. "Take them back down the hill to their fort."

Then he turned to Justice. "You'll need to guard your project more carefully," he instructed Justice. "Remember that the inquisition holds great powers over your devices and can call up your work despite your precautions."

"I'm confused," Justice said. "How do you know of my project? How has it come to your attention that you should warn me thus?"

"The group who barred you from your workplace earlier today was there at my behest," Cernon answered. He looked at Ian as well. "Ian knew we were coming up and kept our secret as requested. He'll need to keep other information from you as they invited him to meet with the Children of Jamari. We'll soon grant you that information as well. Then there will no longer need be no barriers between the two of you."

Cernon looked to Berkhold next. "I approve Justice for visiting our forest anytime he wishes, though I still restrict him to only the first league up from the village. I'll add it to your watch duties to see that he's kept safe while here, as well as helping him to learn our ways."

Berkhold nodded his acceptance.

Cernon looked at Justice again. "We'll keep your secrets. We'll even help you share them out when the time comes."

From Jamari and the Manhood Rites

Jamari came in to dinner tired after a long day walking the tunnels and halls of Milltown Hall. He spotted Shane sitting with Carson and Dan. When they saw him, they all stopped talking and stared. He came to a sudden stop, checking his clothes for tears or holes, checking his hair for hanging strands of cobweb. "What," he finally asked? "What did I do?"

Shane looked around at the small group. "Come on over and have a seat," he said. "I don't think you've done anything, but you've got a bit of a surprise coming." He reached for the pitcher on the table and filled a glass with a clear and sweet-looking wine. "Here, have a drink of this Pinot Gris." He waited while Jamari took a careful sip. "We have another appointment with Doc tomorrow," he said.

"Um . . . I don't get it," Jamari said. "I thought we had all the tests taken care of, but I don't see what the big deal is. You guys act as if someone died or something."

They all exchanged glances. "What?" Jamari exclaimed.

Shane patted him on the leg. "We're probably making you nervous," he said. "It's nothing earth-shattering. It's just, well, most of us have to wait at least a full year, before we're called up for . . ." He paused, visibly trying to find the right words.

"Just say it!" Jamari ordered. "What's going on?"

"Okay," Shane said. "We're going to see Doc tomorrow to so he can clear you for your first breeding experience. He's going to look you over again to make sure you haven't contracted some crazy disease in the last two months and then we're going to show you how to be with a woman."

Jamari was visibly shaken. "I . . . wow. I really thought I'd be a lot older before I had to do that! Why now? Why me? What does it mean?" He took a generous drink of the wine as he absorbed the momentous news. "What if, I mean, if, I can't 'perform' for a woman? What happens to me then?"

"It'll be okay, Jay," Shane answered. "That particular failure happens to all of us at some point in our lives, even when we're with other guys. I've heard it happens more often once you get older than when you're young like we are though. I'm pretty sure that you'll be able to 'perform' as needed. I remember right before my first time that I was nervous too. Back then they had a training program where they had another guy take the role of the woman and then we learned the things we needed to do to make it work out. What we do these days is to have your mentor there in the room with you to guide you through the actions. He . . . I . . . will make sure that you can perform. I know most, if not all, of your trigger points to arousal by now and I'll be able to help."

Shane paused and looked around at the others at the table. Each nodded their assent to some unspoken question as he looked at him. "We've decided that we're going to give you the lessons that we had back then too. Dan is here for a couple reasons. One, he will probably get called up soon for a breeding lesson too. Another is . . . well, he's built right down there so that he'll be best able to mimic a woman during one of the two positions that you'll be learning to carry out."

Jamari looked at Dan with fresh interest. He was thin, thinner than Jamari, who considered himself too thin. His hair was black, but not the jet-black Asian-black, nor the Native American black. His hair had waves still visible even with the short hair of the newly shorn young man's cut.

He had visible muscle tone and his pale skin showed the blue of veins underneath, somehow making him seem frail or vulnerable. Jamari remembered seeing a picture in Matthew's rooms one day of a marble statue carved by some artist named Michelangelo. The statue was called 'The David,' and looking at Dan now, he saw an amazing likeness in the face and how his hair was curled. He had another sip of his wine and thought of another concern. "What if I like it too much?" he asked. "What if I become a breeder, like those outsiders? Will I be kicked out of The Tribe?"

"C'mon, Jay," Shane answered. "Every single adult in The Tribe has been through this before. It won't make you sick. You won't suddenly become 'a breeder'. And here's another one you haven't asked about yet: you won't have to puke, either during or afterward. Just breathe for a minute. And have another sip of wine.

"We're going to make sure you know enough to represent the Young Men's Hall with pride and purpose. You'll be able to enjoy it, just like humans have since they became aware of 'sex' as a separate act from breeding.

"Let's get your dinner over and we can all go to your room for the lessons. We'll all have a good night and then tomorrow you'll be ready to perform with at least a rudimentary ability!"

Back in Jamari's room, Shane took charge of the affair, sending Carson and Dan off on an errand and taking Jamari back into the bedroom to wait. He went into Jamari's closet and took a robe off a hanger and handed it to Jamari. "Take your clothes off. Everything. And put this on." He watched as Jamari complied.

Jamari was still concerned. Once he had his clothes off, he saw that his penis was shriveled to the smallest it had been outside of skinny dipping in the icy waters of the gravel pit. His sack was drawn up tight, bringing his testicles up inside his abdomen. Classic 'fight or flight' symptoms as he'd learned during his martial lessons throughout his entire life. He looked over at Shane with obvious concern.

Shane held Jamari in a long hug, giving him a reassuring squeeze on his butt before breaking away. "Go ahead and put the robe on," he instructed Jamari. "It'll be okay, really. Carson and I have each been through this several times with multiple women. Each of us will be able to tell you what the various possibilities might be like. The basics are the easiest to convey though. Once Carson gets back with the other robes, we'll cover the basic first steps and then walk you through your first penetration.

"We're going to show you some activities earlier than planned tonight, only because you're going to learn things you'll need to know tomorrow. Which is also earlier than planned as well. After this though, you will still have to wait through the normal process before we can show more of what you'll see the beginning of tonight. I'm talking in circles, I know. Just trust me and go along with it okay?"

"Yeah," Jamari answered as he settled the robe onto his shoulders. "What's with the way this hangs?" he asked about the robe. "It's like it's wide open starting at the crotch, not likely to keep me warm at all." He tried to adjust the simple brown robe to cover his inner thighs and couldn't get it to reach at all.

"That's not its function," Shane answered. "This is a breeding robe. It's designed to allow the women to get your semen without having to have full body contact. You'll see. I think I heard Carson come back a bit ago. Let me look." He went over to the door and partially opened it to peek out. "Okay, they're ready," he said. "C'mon in you two."

www.ingramcontent.com/pod-product-compliance
Lightning Source LLC
Chambersburg PA
CBHW051250160726
47994CB00003B/1106